THE LEVITICUS RATS EXPERIMENT

A THINKING PERSON'S SCIENCE FICTION STORY

MICHAEL GROSSMAN

authorHOUSE

AuthorHouse™
1663 Liberty Drive
Bloomington, IN 47403
www.authorhouse.com
Phone: 833-262-8899

Published by AuthorHouse 01/19/2024

ISBN: 979-8-8230-1973-6 (sc)
ISBN: 979-8-8230-1974-3 (hc)
ISBN: 979-8-8230-1972-9 (e)

Library of Congress Control Number: 2023924438

Print information available on the last page.

For my dad, Milton,
and my kids, Alyson and Zachary

I have had enough of the offerings of ... well-fed beasts; I do
not delight in the blood of bulls, or of lambs, or of goats.
—Isaiah 1:11 (Isaiah lived ca. 740–701 BCE)

No animal from the herd or from the flock shall be slaughtered
on the same day as its young [i.e., no cow, ewe or goat shall die
with the killing of her young the last thing she laid eyes on].
—Leviticus 22:28 (written sixth century BCE)

Six days thou shalt do thy work, but on the seventh day thou
shalt rest, that thine ox and thine ass may have rest.
—Exodus 23:12 (written sixth century BCE)

Thou shalt not muzzle the ox that treadeth out the
corn [i.e., so it can eat while treading].
—Deuteronomy 25:4 (written seventh century BCE)

Surely the fate of humans is like that of animals; the same fate awaits
them. As one dies, so does the other. All have the same breath. ... All
go to the same place; all come from dust, and to dust all return.
—Ecclesiastes 3:19–20 (written ca. 450 BCE)

The use of animals in medical research and safety testing is
a vital part of the quest to improve human health. It always
has been and probably always will be, despite the alternatives
available. ... Without animal testing, there will be no new
drugs for new or hard-to-treat diseases. ... Animal research is
an essential part of compassionate humanistic endeavor.
—*The Lancet* 364 (2004), pp. 815–16

Contents

Acknowledgments

The Gary Schwartz character in *The Leviticus Rats Experiment* is based on the real Gary E. Schwartz, whom I met at Canyon Ranch Resort, Arizona, in 2007 and again in 2009. Although I've tried to be accurate when describing his career and accomplishments, most of what I've written, particularly about his early education and research involving laboratory rats, is purely fictional.

In the last section of chapter 30, I have drawn heavily from an article by Julie Redstone titled "Moving toward Fifth-Dimensional Awareness" (*Light Times*, June 2008). Almost all the ideas and metaphors in that section are hers.

The description of the incredible "whispering" ability of John Solomon Rarey (1827–1866) and the events of his life, set forth in chapter 33, are drawn from Nicholas Evans's book *The Horse Whisperer* (Delacorte, 1995). I often paraphrased or used what he wrote without much alteration.

In the epilogue, I've set forth scientific information I gleaned from multiple sources on the internet to prove that the forces at play described in *The Leviticus Rats Experiment* are real or one day could be. I've mostly just reworded and reorganized that information and then inserted several paragraphs of my own ideas.

Also, in the section of my epilogue titled "Traveling at the Speed of Light and Faster," the analogy of the bunched-up carpet I use to explain Alcubierre warp drive is from Michio Kaku's book *Parallel Worlds* (Anchor, 2005).

Disclaimers

Although nothing described in *The Leviticus Rats Experiment* is beyond the possible, the events and characters I've written about, except as mentioned in my acknowledgments, are all fictional. In particular, the research I describe at the University of Vermont and Acharya Jagadish Chandra College in Calcutta never really happened. And Burlington and Calcutta are not even nearly as rodent infested as I've suggested.

Also, the dates of the Bible passages I quote are approximate since historians widely differ as to the correct dates. In addition, the wording of those passages may not be the same as in the particular Bible you read since there exist at least a hundred English translations of the Bible from the ancient languages—Aramaic, Hebrew, and Greek—it was first written in.

Foreword

The subtitle of *The Leviticus Rats Experiment* is A *Thinking Person's Science Fiction Story*. If you merely skim-read as you would a post on TikTok, Reddit, or Snapchat, I do not think you will fully take in all the details of the incredible phenomena it describes. These days, we have become so accustomed to receiving our information, or misinformation, from the internet that many of us have lost our ability to concentrate when we read and to think deeply about what we've read. I therefore urge you to slow down and read with concentration the pages that follow. If you do, I think you will enjoy this story almost as much as I enjoyed writing it. If you get confused or lost in the details once in a while, see the glossary at the back. Also, be sure to read the epilogue, which is an integral part of this story.

· *

I have always been interested in science, but I became passionately interested, and decided to write a science fiction story, while doing legal work for a company involved in biomedical research. The experiments that company participated in, to find new drugs to treat maladies for which there are still no effective cures, fascinated me. I am certain that kind of work is far more important than the legal work I did negotiating and drafting contracts.

My passion drove me to read everything I could lay my hands on about the life sciences: Charles Darwin's theory of evolution, Gregor Mendel's laws of dominant and recessive genes, Watson and Crick's double helix structure of DNA, and other famous scientists' discoveries, such as those of Marie Curie, Rachel Carson, Louis Pasteur, and Richard Dawkins.

I eventually grew confident enough to tackle what I consider more difficult subjects like physics and astronomy, including quantum mechanics and, in particular, the big bang theory of how the universe, its stars, and its trillions of planets were created, some of which can sustain life, which constantly evolves and sometimes mutates into new species.

The Leviticus Rats Experiment is my end product.

PART I

THE HAND WAVERS

Chapter 1

There were 2,860 of them packed so tightly together that they could not stretch their extremities more than a centimeter. And they were drenched with each other's sweat. It was dark, like belowdecks on a slave ship, and they were tethered, not by straps, but by the unrelenting pressure of their bodies pressing against one another. There was no ventilation, and the stench of their urine permeated everything like a thick, putrid smog. Although they were incapable of speaking even a syllable of their masters' tongue, the meaning of the sounds they made could not be mistaken for anything but pleas for mercy. These unfortunate souls had no God to pray to for relief because they had no religion, and where they had been collected, the book of Leviticus—and any biblical book for that matter—was unknown.

Professor Simona Gupta saw through her high-definition Bushnell binoculars that the specially designed transport carrying these souls was stuck in an impossible traffic jam nearly two miles away. She easily spotted it from the high-level office she'd been provided in the University of Vermont's Biomedical Research Building because the driver, Ralph Crider, six foot seven and powerfully built, had climbed atop the cab to see what was blocking things. Gupta tried to get his attention by radioing, but there was no signal. She tried calling his cell phone, but again, there was no signal.

The temperature had topped out at 105 degrees but wasn't dropping. If the four-car collision holding up traffic wasn't cleared soon, the entire cargo might die or become so enervated that it would be useless for any research. Crider, desperate, climbed down from the cab and, using his enormous strength, began pushing the cars ahead of him to the shoulder of the road.

"Aubrey, get over there," Gupta shouted. "Take my car and bring that new tech Ron Carter with you. Use the back road through Westfield, get as close as you can, and then walk if you have to, but get to our damn truck.

That cargo cost our investors half a million, and if it dies, our whole project is kaput. We'll never get enough financing to start over again."

Gupta was one of the foremost biomedical researchers in the world. She'd discovered cures for two types of cancer, helped perfect procedures for organ transplant, and successfully grown human ears using stem cells. Her current passion was trying to find a cure for diabetes, which in this century was an epidemic and had killed millions more than COVID-19. Aubrey Adams, although decades younger, was Gupta's best and, by far, her most talented assistant.

"I'm leaving now," Aubrey said. "Give me your car keys. I'll bring the portable generator we keep in our parking lot to reboot the AC and a dolly to wheel it up on. But that generator weighs five hundred pounds, and in this heat, I don't think just Carter and I will be able to push it. I'll ask Bob Morris to come with us." Bob was another of Gupta's assistants.

The live cargo had sat sweltering for hours in scores of small, ridiculously overcrowded housings, about twelve tiny beings stuffed into each on tiers of shelves within Ralph Crider's truck. Although specially designed and equipped to carry living things, the truck's Wi-Fi, ventilation, and cooling systems had malfunctioned, as had the watering system for all these housings, each of which normally held six small creatures at most. Crider, in a last-ditch effort to save his cargo, crammed double that number into every housing where the water had not totally evaporated. Fortunately, when Aubrey, Carter, and Morris arrived, they were able to quickly connect the generator. The AC kicked on, and the cargo began to slowly revive.

The slave ship–like truck with a logo reading "Direct Services" on both sides finally arrived at the university. There it was gently unloaded, and the live cargo was transferred to more comfortable quarters, in which the ventilation, lighting, watering, and all other life support systems worked perfectly.

At the time, the one who would become their leader, whom Gupta later named Larry, was as frightened and helpless as the rest.

Chapter 2

It came upon him gradually, but until recently, Larry had been feeling lousy. So had his five roommates, but they were feeling better too. Larry, who seemed more intelligent than the others, often discussed the affliction they had all suffered, but he did so using a strange language only they could understand.

Shortly after they moved into their new quarters, one by one, they'd become ill—not from a virus or any infectious disease, but as they eventually figured out, from stress. Small lab creatures, like Larry, are always susceptible to stress which, if the stress became severe, sometimes causes their capillaries to hemorrhage. Doctors or, more accurately, laboratory technicians constantly tended to them, but no one could stop their bleeding.

A few weeks back, however, some men and women started gently waving their hands over the lab creatures, often for as long as a half hour at a time. The motion of their hands, somehow, was very calming. The same people would do this almost daily. Larry and his roommates were not the only ill ones. All the residents in the quarters on the same floor were feeling sick. Other men and women started moving their hands over the residents in the quarters next to Larry's too. But the effect was not the same. Those residents remained unhealthy, and some worsened and died. Larry and all his roommates, however, dramatically improved.

After a month of hand-waving, the hundreds of hemorrhaging blood vessels that had afflicted Larry and his roommates miraculously healed. Only Professor Gupta and the doctor who had dreamed up the hand-waving treatment understood why.

For you and me to understand, we have to first understand something else. The people who moved their hands over Larry's quarters were professional energy healers. Many were Native Americans, some were from the Far East, and a few were aging hippies from the Woodstock generation, but all had been trained in something called energy medicine. They believed, with scientific evidence to back it up, that all living things emanate energy fields, *auras* if you will, that can be adjusted by skilled energy-healing practitioners. These practitioners have learned to direct the auras emanating from themselves powerfully enough to interact with the auras of their sick patients.

The people who moved their hands over the residents in the quarters next to Larry's, however, were not professional energy healers at all, just regular Joes with no training or experience in energy medicine whatsoever. They had agreed to try but didn't hold themselves out to be energy healers. And most didn't even know what energy healing was.

Gary Schwartz, the doctor who had thought up the hand-waving, had decided to let the real healers treat Larry and his roommates and let the regular Joes treat the residents in the adjacent quarters. He kept detailed records. He found that the real healers were able to stop the bleeding nearly 95 percent of the time, whereas the regular Joes stopped it only 15 percent of the time. The residents who were untreated—that is, in quarters on Larry's floor where no one, not even regular Joes, waved their hands at them—continued to bleed at the same rate.

But why did the regular Joes have any success?

"Maybe," Dr. Schwartz surmised, "because even these untrained sham healers were able to direct their auras at the sick residents forcefully enough once in a while and focus them enough to have a slight effect. Maybe some of the sham healers, though they have no training, were natural healers without knowing it."

The Native American healers told Dr. Schwartz they had expected that their hand-waving would be at least somewhat successful, and they were only a bit surprised by the dramatic results. But Dr. Schwartz, who was not an energy healer and still not even sure he believed in energy healing, was astonished. To him, the improvement in the health of Larry and his roommates was incredible, but he couldn't deny the results of his own experiment.

In fact, he expanded his experiment and brought the healers to the sick residents living everywhere on Larry's floor, and the effect was always the same. The sham hand-wavers stopped the bleeding only a few times, while the genuine hand-wavers stopped it most of the time.

Doctor Schwartz had heard of energy medicine and had become interested in it long before he decided to let its practitioners have a crack at Larry and his roommates' bleeding blood vessels. He'd always suspected that there might really be something to it because a few widely accepted healing systems like acupuncture and magnetic wave therapy, for examples, were thought to work because the insertion of needles or placement of magnets at strategic points on people's bodies could redirect the flow of energy traveling along invisible channels within us. All people have energy flowing through such channels, and illnesses are often caused when the energy flows become out of whack. The illnesses can be cured by bringing the flows back to normal.

But to fully appreciate why the real hand-wavers were so incredibly effective, you have to realize another thing. If you haven't quite figured it out yet, you have to realize that not only were the real hand-wavers skilled energy-healing practitioners, but also that Larry is not human, nor a miniature humanlike being in any shape, fashion, or form. He is not a miniature Neanderthal-like or Cro-Magnon–like creature either, somehow brought back to life from DNA frozen in glaciers. Nor is he a miniature monkey or a miniature advanced primate. On the mammal scale, he is on the very low end. Larry, in fact, is a six-inch-long rat.

All his roommates and all the residents living on his floor are rats, and their quarters are not apartments but one-and-a-half-foot-high, two-foot-long plastic cages. On Larry's floor alone there are 470 of these cages. On the floors above and below Larry's, the residents are hamsters, mice, guinea pigs, rabbits, and even cats and dogs—all laboratory animals specially bred for use in biomedical research.

Larry and his roommates were very specially bred, a genus known as *Rattus norvegicus diabetica*, that is, brown diabetic rats. This genus had been bred so that the rats would always be born with type 1 diabetes and researchers worldwide could use them to try to find a cure. In addition to testing new kinds of insulin on these rats, researchers try gene implantation. Rats can mate as early as three months old, so if a gene is implanted into the diabetic parents of litter 1, then within the same year scientists can see what effect the implantation has had four generations later. They constantly try to implant different genes to see if the diabetes the *Rattus norvegicus diabetica* were born with can be bred out. The same gene tweaking can be done with rats bred to be born with heart disease, certain types of cancer, deafness, blindness, Crohn's disease, Parkinson's disease, you name it.

A drawback of using rats for biomedical research is that their confinement always causes stress, and after a while that stress, as previously mentioned, can cause blood vessels in the rats' bodies to start rupturing. That is what happened to Larry and every rat on his floor after six months of confinement. And that rupturing was what Larry frequently discussed with his cage-mates. Remarkably, after the energy healers had started their hand-waving, Larry somehow knew it was the hand-waving that was healing his blood vessels. More incredibly, he knew why it was working.

The stress and bleeding could be dealt with in ways other than by energy medicine. Larry knew that too because he'd seen with his own eyes other treatments administered in the animal lab at the University of Vermont (UVM). Medications sometimes worked, injected or oral. So did forced sleep, induced by anesthesia. But those methods were invasive, whereas the energy healing method was not. The hand-wavers never even handled (no pun intended) the rats, touching not a hair on their bodies. One of the reasons energy healing works so well on small rats is because the hand-wavers' energy fields are so massive compared to the rats' that the healers are able to powerfully impact the rats' auras.

At six inches long, Larry was just average size for a *Rattus norvegicus diabetica*, and nothing about him seemed different from any of the other rats. But as the days passed, the laboratory technicians took note of his increasingly thick and lustrous chestnut-colored fur, his penetrating large eyes, the dexterity with which he could use his four paws, and the thing that perplexed them most, the multiple humanlike expressions he could make with his face. Until Doctor Gary Schwartz came along, energy medicine as a treatment for stress in lab animals had never been tried. His experiment was successful beyond all expectations, but obviously it had some strange side effects.

Which brings us back to this: How was it that Larry knew what was happening to him? How was it that he could talk with his cage-mates about what was happening? And why did he seem much more intelligent than the other rats, with the expressions on his face being almost human?

Chapter 3

Whatever incomprehensible combination of squeaks and snarls rats use to communicate, Larry became the best at it by far. His closest friend *Rattus norvegicus diabetca 5* – he didn't have a name, just a number – could understand Larry and have detailed conversations with him but spoke with tremendous difficulty and much more haltingly. Even so, aside from Larry, he was the most perceptive rat in the entire building although there was clearly a great distance between the two. He had coarser, dirtier looking fur; crookeder, yellower, and more worn teeth; much beadier, though not unfriendly eyes; obviously functioned on a much slower level, and often had a completely blank and dull, rather stupid expression on his face. We'll give him the name *R-Five* to distinguish him from the other cage-mates, *Rattus norvegicus diabetcas 1, 2, 3* and *4,* who were even duller. Larry's number, surprisingly, was *6* which, but for his special qualities, made him low man on the totem pole.

After the energy healers had finished their job and left, having brought the hemorrhaging blood vessels of almost all the rats under control, the first to notice how differently Larry had started behaving were Aubrey and Becky Byers. Becky was another of Gupta's assistants. Both she and Aubrey were laboratory animal technologists (LATGs) who were very involved in the diabetes research project the rats were being used for at UVM. Becky was the project's animal colony manager, and Aubrey was her right-hand woman. Twelve other technicians, of whom three were laboratory animal technicians (LATs) and of whom nine were assistant laboratory animal technicians (ALATs), reported to Becky and were responsible for tasks such as feeding the rats, cleaning their cages, maintaining a constant temperature, and treating minor wounds. There were also several assistant veterinarians (vet techs) on staff who performed more complicated procedures such as putting the animals under anesthesia to extract broken or decayed teeth.

Most importantly, as per the instructions of Gupta's diabetes research colleague Robert Tompkins, a professor who had created a revolutionary new kind of insulin, they followed the schedule he'd given them to a T by injecting exact amounts of his new insulin, at exact injection sites on the rats' bodies, at exact times every day.

It turned out to be incredibly effective and, with Gupta's help, eventually made the rats' diabetically high glucose levels drop to normal.

Even so, the injections pissed off Larry tremendously. They pissed off all the rats. Although the shots weren't painful—the ALATs, LATs, and vet techs had been trained to administer them in such a way as to avoid causing pain—they certainly contributed to the stress that had brought on the hemorrhaging blood vessels.

R-Five was the first to complain about it, which was surprising because the unthinking, dull expression on his face rarely lifted. By forcing himself to always keep a stupid looking mien, and often intentionally mumble, it was if he was trying to conceal the true extent of his intelligence from the other rats and especially from Larry.

A few weeks after the rats had been delivered to UVM, he said, "Larry, I do not th … think we can st … stand these sh … shots mu … much lon … longer. We are all ble … bleeding." By then all his cage-mates could speak fluently and *Rattus norvegicus diabetica 3* added, in nearly grammatically perfect rat dialect, "Every morning when I wake up, clumps of my hair are matted together. I think it's dried blood. We've got to make them stop!"

Larry, who after the hand-waving had started was usually the most garrulous, replied simply, "Don't worry, I'm planning something."

Aubrey was the first to sense that the rats were communicating. She'd watch them for hours and see their mouths moving, and it dawned on her that they might actually be talking. She reported this to Becky, and they both told Professor Tompkins. They didn't dare do that again because the next day he wrote them up. If they hadn't told him later that they were only joking, he would have fired them.

*

You'll likely think it a paradox, but almost all people involved in biomedical research using lab animals are animal lovers. They are trained by the American Association for Laboratory Animal Science (AALAS), the meaning of whose motto, "Refinement, Reduction, and Replacement (the Three R's)," is that laboratory scientists should refine experiments so they cause no pain, reduce the number of animals needed, and replace the animals with tissue samples or computer models whenever possible. At AALAS national conventions, which are held annually and attended by thousands of lab animal technicians and veterinarians, scores of classes are held on technical subjects and on the ethical and legal responsibilities of biomedical researchers.

Federal law is extremely demanding when it comes to lab animals and at facilities where they are used, such as UVM, requires that an ethics committee be set up to ensure that the Three R's are being strictly followed. The committee must include a scientist familiar with the use of research animals, a veterinarian on call to treat the animals, and a nonscientist animal welfare representative, who is often a priest, rabbi, or minister. The committee's sole purpose is to protect the animals, and if it determined that any of the Three R's has been violated, it has authority to shut down even a multimillion-dollar research project.

People for Ethical Treatment of Animals (PETA) might disagree, but most lab animal techs are nearly as militant about animal rights activism as they are. In fact, sometimes the treatments lab animal techs discover work better on animal diseases than on human ones. Some of the lab animal techs, moreover, are themselves card-carrying members of PETA.

Larry and his cage-mates couldn't care less whether Aubrey, Becky, or any of the techs thought they were helping animals while they did experiments to find cures for human maladies. Whoop-de-doo that occasionally a cancer drug would work on dogs, but not on people. As time passed, the rats became increasingly more resentful of constantly being poked with needles even though their diabetes had all but disappeared. As Larry put it, "We're tired of being treated like we're guinea pigs." He said that aloud as Aubrey watched, and although she couldn't understand—she didn't speak rat—every rat in Larry's cage and every rat on his floor, even the stupidest, knew exactly what he meant. They had become intelligent enough to easily understand his quip.

Chapter 4

Obviously, something beyond the extraordinary had happened. Let's review: Larry, a *Rattus norvegicus diabetica* lab rat, being treated with Professor Tompkins's new insulin, was feeling lousy, not because of the constant injections, but because of hemorrhaging blood vessels brought on by stress. The hemorrhaging had stopped after Doctor Schwartz thought to have energy healers wave their hands over the rats, but with the strange side effect of causing Larry to become intelligent, as had his cage-mates, albeit to a lesser extent. They had become so intelligent that they developed the ability to talk to each other. That was why the cage-mates were able to comprehend Larry's very sophisticated—for a rodent anyway—witticism, "We're tired of being treated like we're guinea pigs."

And now that the hemorrhaging blood vessels were no longer a problem and Tompkins's new insulin had almost totally cured their diabetes, the *Rattus norvegicus diabetica* rats had become increasingly resentful of the frequent shots. Moreover, *Rattus norvegicus diabetica 1–4* and R-Five had become perceptive enough to complain to Larry about them and were reassured when he responded, "Don't worry, I'm planning something."

Larry had become so intelligent that he understood how he had become intelligent.

The energy fields—auras—of energy healers were barely detectable, but they were indeed detectable by other living things. After years of practice, these healers had learned how to direct their auras and focus them to such an extent that they interacted powerfully with their patients' auras. These healers couldn't perform an appendectomy, for example, that way but they could begin to heal a disease such as cancer and sometimes even cure it.

Now imagine an exceptionally gifted energy healer with an exceptionally powerful aura standing over some small rats and ministering to them. Under the right circumstances, that could have a permanent effect on the rats' tiny auras. That's what happened to Larry and, to a lesser degree, all the rats ministered to by the healers. Larry had been an unusually intelligent rat to begin with because even before the hand-wavers had come along, he had much denser gray matter than ordinary rats. He'd inherited the DNA for dense gray matter from his great-great-grandparents whose cerebral genes had been tweaked in an experiment to find a cure for Alzheimer's. The same gene tweaking that had caused Larry to have denser gray matter and therefore had caused him to be more intelligent than normal rats had also caused his aura to become exceedingly sensitive.

Moxus, a Native American and the most talented of the healers, always positioned himself close to Larry and projected his aura mostly at him. Larry absorbed a huge portion of that aura into his own, and the two auras combined into one exponentially magnified energy field.

If we could have observed this process unfolding, then before Moxus ministered to him, we would have seen Larry's aura as a dry potted plant on a windowsill, thirsting for moisture and then, after being watered, bursting to life. We'd have observed its stems rapidly twisting and thickening as they grew, its leaves regreening, and its flowers blooming in fantastically vivid colors and intricate patterns.

That's how the combined auras of Moxus and Larry, that is, their incredibly magnified energy field, would have appeared if we had the ability to see it. And when Moxus left, the incredibly powerful energy field didn't leave with him. It remained with Larry, and after a time, this heretofore insignificant *Rattus norvegicus diabetica* learned how to use it.

One night as Larry was drifting off to sleep, the number 3,145.42 popped into his mind. He didn't know why it had appeared, but on a whim, he multiplied it by 5,280 and effortlessly came up with the correct product: 16,607,817.6. He had done it instantly, like a savant able to solve a math problem faster than a calculator, and realized that he'd just computed the correct distance, in feet, between Burlington, Vermont, and the North Pole. He could do other calculations, more difficult and more complex, and easily compute the distance between Burlington and anywhere, including the Moon, Mars, the Sun, and even other galaxies.

Larry's aura did not remain static. Its power increased daily, and it wasn't long before he learned to do more than just calculate numbers.

When Aubrey and Becky came by, he'd project his aura toward them. After doing this, he found that he could sense their thoughts, like Counselor Deanna Troi's ability to sense the thoughts of the entire crew of the starship *Enterprise*. Unlike Deanna, however, Larry developed the ability not only to sense, but also to read, in minute detail, every thought in the mind of any creature he focused on.

Larry's mental abilities continued increasing, and his aura was soon able to influence the thoughts of animals and people wherever they were on his floor. In fact, less than a month after his aura had combined with Moxus's, he found he could *control every thought and every action* of nearly every living thing in the entire building.

So, when Larry told his cage-mates he had a plan to deal with the injections that they resented so much, he wasn't kidding. He realized that his incredible energy field gave him the ability to do things that no lab tech, veterinarian, researcher, or healer ever could do or could even imagine ever doing.

*

In terms of Simona Gupta's credentials, she had earned PhD's in biochemistry, anatomy, and zoology, and was professor of interdisciplinary life sciences and dean of the Biomedical Research Department at UVM, where she spent most of her time, residing on campus. She was also a part-time professor and researcher in Calcutta, India, at Acharya Jagadish Chandra College (AJCC), testing new drugs on advanced primates. The use of such animals in the United States was being phased out, and using them for new experiments was now illegal.

Gupta, fifty-five years old, had never married and had never been involved in a long-term relationship, and therefore she was able to devote all her energy and as much time as necessary to pursuing her life's work, including—and above all—her efforts to cure diabetes.

Gupta often instructed her students, "Although insulin resistance in people afflicted with diabetes is extremely common, total resistance is very rare. For insulin-resistant people, the kinds of injected insulin currently on the market don't work. These people walk around with enormously high concentrations of glucose in their bloodstreams, which causes plaque to build up, which eventually blocks their arteries, veins, and capillaries, hindering them from circulating blood. Too frequently, amputation of the toes or feet becomes necessary, or the individual goes blind, or develops kidney, heart, or other organ failure. Of the several hundred million diabetics alive around the world today, many millions are near death mostly because of their insulin resistance."

Gupta, as mentioned, had helped Professor Robert Tompkins formulate his new insulin, which she dubbed PRT in his honor. Together, they had decided to start testing it on diabetic gorillas and chimpanzees at AJCC.

Gupta had been instrumental in developing a sign language to communicate with these gorillas and chimps. She learned that they were capable of complex thought on a much higher level than researchers had suspected. Amazingly, although apes were naturally far more intelligent than rats, the intelligence of the *Rattus norvegicus diabetica* at UVM, which had developed due to the hand-waving of the energy healers, had surpassed and become vastly superior to that of any ape that had ever lived.

But Tompkins's PRT, although effective at causing the *Rattus norvegicus diabetica* at UVM to overcome their insulin resistance and lowering their high glucose levels to normal, had not been successful at doing the same for the apes at AJCC. PRT, therefore, was a long way from being ready for Gupta and Tompkins's ultimate goal: human testing. They both worried that it might never be ready and had repeatedly broken promises to their investors that tests on human subjects would begin soon.

They worried, like all researchers unable to demonstrate successful results, that their investors would cut off their funding.

Chapter 5

One, Two, Three, and Four; R-Five; and Larry, whose number was six, huddled together in their cage on the last few square inches of wood shavings not yet saturated with their own piss and shit. Before they had become intelligent, they looked forward each day to licking the excrement from each other's fur, but now that they could think, they couldn't bear the stench alone, to say nothing of the taste.

Although the UVM lab was equipped with an elaborate cage-cleaning system that ran each cage through a soapy spray on a conveyor belt to wash away the pissed-on and shit-on wood chips; scrub and disinfect the cage; and replace the old wood chips, it had broken down and been out of service for days.

Rattus norvegicus diabetica 3 said to no one in particular, "I wonder what Larry's been up to. He's been in his own world for days."

R-Five, in his usual slow and halting manner, replied "I'm, uh ... I'm not cer ... certain, Three, but some ... something's go ... going on."

One, Two, Three, Four, and R-Five had grown a bit cautious of Larry because they were very aware of his aura's ever-increasing strength. This was why they tried to avoid complaining about anything directly to his face and often spoke in third person, hoping that expressing their concerns this way would spare them his anger.

Four said, "I hope something is done soon to get the techs to clean up our cage [he didn't dare say, "I hope Larry does something"] and stop these shots. If Aubrey gives me one more, I'll kill myself."

Two added, "Of all the techs, she's the gentlest. Her shots don't hurt much. But still, I don't like these LATGs, LATs, or ALATs, or whatever they call themselves, touching me all the time. Sometimes they're careless, and when they are, the injections hurt a lot."

Aubrey was watching. She was certain the rats were talking, but she immediately shoved aside any thought of bringing it to Professor

Tompkins's attention again. If she were to do so, he'd fire her on the spot, and her career as an LATG would be over. He'd see to it that no research institution in the country would ever hire her.

If Aubrey had been privy to R-Five and his cage-mates' conversation, she'd have been horrified. She deeply believed that causing lab animals the slightest amount of unnecessary pain was a crime, if not legally, then ethically. At AALAS conventions, she'd lectured on the Three R's, feeling that the violation of any one of them was unforgivable. Aubrey always took care of her animals before taking care of herself. She'd taken to heart the biblical commandment "A man must not eat his meal before giving food to his cattle" (Tractate Berachot 40a).

Even more than horrified to discover that the insulin shots sometimes caused the rats pain, she'd be dumbfounded at the extent of their ability to communicate. She and Becky figured that maybe the rats, from being confined together in a small cage and forced into close physical contact all the time, just appeared to be talking and were merely signaling their growing discomfort by squeaking and snarling at each other—like they always did—more often.

But in complete sentences? waiting for one rat to stop making sounds before another would begin to? And expressing complex feelings? If she'd known, she'd have had her head examined.

*

By now, a full two months after the healers had left, Larry's aura had grown so powerful that he could do much more than read and influence the thoughts of the animals and people around him. He'd developed the ability to alter their very physiology, albeit minutely and only in increments. It started as just a game. He'd slowly cause his cage-mates' tails to grow longer, their teeth to become sharper, and sometimes the pupils of their eyes to grow larger so they could see better. He did little things like that to impress them, until he realized he could even make their brains grow larger.

And he didn't hesitate. He bathed all the rats in his cage, including himself, in his exponentially magnified energy field, and almost perceptibly the gray matter of their cerebral cortexes, cerebrums, and cerebellums became thicker and denser. After his cage-mates had become totally fluent in rat language, he stopped enlarging their gray matter, but continued enlarging his own. He became more intelligent than even the brightest researcher on staff. Compared to him, Doctor Schwartz and Professors Gupta and Tompkins were like, well, laboratory rats.

Unfortunately, Larry had also become arrogant and quite disdainful of the lesser beings around him. But he was never cruel, and the thought of harming any living creature, including a human, never crossed his mind. That could easily change, however, if the reptilian portions of his brain, that is, his brain stem, basal ganglia, and cerebellum, which together controlled basic instincts such as territorial behavior, aggression, and sex drive, continued growing larger.

But for now, as the days passed, Larry and *Rattus norvegicus diabetica 1–4* became closer and closer companions, even though Larry's intellect was ridiculously superior to theirs because of the huge amount of gray matter that had accumulated in his cerebral cortex. And more important than this, his friendship with R-Five deepened.

Chapter 6

Despite his awesome abilities, Larry's first plan to fend off the annoying PRT injections failed. He knew that all *Rattus norvegicus diabetica* required at least some insulin to survive, so he didn't want to eliminate the shots entirely, having realized that Tompkins's new insulin was potent enough that a single shot every few days would do. One night Larry began to plant suggestions into the mind of vet tech Bob Morris, saying that he had already given the shot that Bob was scheduled administer the next morning. Although the suggestion sank in, the plan failed because there were a half dozen safeguards in place to prevent an injection from ever being missed.

Morris was supposed to inject Larry and his cage-mates at exactly eight thirty each morning and thereafter at six-hour intervals. At twenty minutes after eight o'clock, he walked toward the cage, but while he was on the way, Larry completed the process of making him think he'd done it already. Larry had begun the process of influencing Bob's thoughts the evening before to ensure that the suggestion would take hold. It did, so Bob turned around, never even reaching the cage. At twenty-five minutes past eight, however, when motion detectors failed to detect the presence of any tech poised to deliver the insulin shots, an alarm went off, and immediately two other techs rushed over and administered them right on schedule.

Larry did not have the ability to affect nonliving, inanimate things and therefore couldn't stop the alarm from sounding. He couldn't affect machinery in any way. He had tried to prevent the other techs from taking Bob Morris's place, but he knew that it would take several hours before people would act on his suggestions. The five minutes between when the alarm had gone off and the other techs rushed over was not enough time to make the techs do anything.

Larry's second plan also failed. This time he had implanted the suggestion that the scheduled morning shot had already been done into the minds of every tech on his floor. When Bob Morris didn't show and the alarm sounded, the suggestions Larry had implanted in the other techs' minds made them think they had already rushed to take Bob's place, even though they hadn't. But three minutes before the deadline, a second alarm went off that could be heard in control rooms all over the building. Several techs from other floors raced to Larry's cage to save the day by administering the shots exactly on time.

Larry was not the least bit discouraged. He devised another plan, one that would implant suggestions into the mind of every ALAT, LAT, LATG, veterinarian, researcher, scientist, and manager in the entire building. That way, no matter how many alarms went off, there'd be no staff anywhere in the building in control of their own thoughts. Everyone would think they'd already given the shots they were supposed to have given, and there'd be no one around to realize they hadn't. That plan would have worked.

But before Larry could implement it, something happened so strange and at odds with the purpose of the diabetes research project that even he himself couldn't comprehend it. The insulin injections suddenly stopped, completely and all at once. Larry had not heard any discussion among the techs about ending them or, more startling, read a single thought about ending them in the mind of anyone, including Tompkins and Gupta. Until then, every rat on Larry's floor, in all four hundred seventy cages, had been given four shots of the same dosage of PRT at the same times every day like clockwork.

*

PRT is remarkable because it works very differently from the kinds of insulin currently available. The dosages of those kinds, which diabetics self-injected, are based on the carbohydrate counts of the meals they are about to consume. The more carbohydrates, the larger the insulin dosage; the fewer carbohydrates, the smaller the dosage. All carbohydrates, no matter how large or small the quantity, ultimately are digested down to glucose. From our stomachs, when digestion is complete, the glucose enters our bloodstreams.

Insulin is the hormone that allows the glucose in our bloodstreams to be absorbed into our cells, where tiny structures called mitochondria transform the glucose into energy. That energy is what enables our brains to think, our hearts to beat, and our arms and legs and everything else to move.

Diabetes develops when the pancreas can't produce enough or any insulin. Type 2 diabetics can produce some, but not enough; type 1's can't produce any. Injections of the man-made currently available insulins function by replacing the natural insulin that a type 1's pancreas has completely stopped making. It's a constant, time-consuming chore to match a correct insulin dose to the carbohydrate count. A mismatch causes severe problems. An insulin dose too large makes the cells absorb too much glucose, rapidly depleting the body of glucose and thereby depriving the body of its energy source. That can cause type 1's to lose consciousness, go into shock, and in rare instances, die. A dose too small leaves high levels of glucose circulating in the blood, which damages veins, arteries, and capillaries, which in turn can cause gangrene, kidney disease, heart failure, and blindness.

All the *Rattus norvegicus diabetica* were type 1's, but their PRT dosages, until the injections suddenly stopped, had always been exactly the same. Not because the carb counts of their meals were always the same—in fact, the carb counts were purposely wildly varied—but because PRT had the incredible quality, once injected, of adjusting its potency depending on the amount of carbohydrates consumed. If the rats had been fed large, high-carb meals, then the PRT automatically became more potent. If they had been small, low-carb meals, then the PRT automatically became less potent. No matter how many carbs a *Rattus norvegicus diabetica* consumed and digested into glucose, Tompkins's insulin caused just the right amount to transfer into the rat's bloodstream. The glucose would then enter its cells, where the mitochondria converted it to energy.

I hope you're still with me. I've given all this background for a reason. You see, just as the hand-waving done by Dr. Schwartz's energy healers had the unforeseen side effect of giving Larry superintelligence and incredible mental abilities, Professor Tompkins's PRT had an unexpected side effect too: the unheard-of ability to self-adjust, *almost as if it could think for itself.*

Chapter 7

Shortly after the injections of Tompkins's insulin began, Larry sensed an invisible presence hovering nearby. He tried to read this presence's thoughts, if it even had any, but he could never pinpoint where it was coming from. At times it seemed to be concentrated in a single location, but at others it seemed everywhere.

This strange presence had been disturbing only when Larry had had the ridiculously low intelligence of a normal rat. It had become less and less disturbing as he grew more and more intelligent because he had come to understand that it had no threatening intentions and was therefore essentially harmless. Still, he could occasionally feel its strength and worried that if provoked, this presence might unleash a power to rival his own.

Larry's cage-mates sensed the presence too. All of them, except R-Five, immediately perked up their ears and sniffed the air when they awoke each morning to see if they could locate it. They never could, and after a while, they stopped being spooked and looking over their shoulders.

R-Five was the only one who seemed totally unaffected by the presence. He gave no sign of even acknowledging it was there, except for when one of the other rats seemed a bit jumpy, at which time the lips on his normally dull face would curve upward into a tiny amused smile.

Aubrey also often felt the presence, and to her, the obvious cause was Tompkins's self-adjusting PRT. Not so obvious was that Tompkins's insulin had morphed into a sentient being within, and dependent upon, the body of each rat it had been injected into. These sentient beings survived by feeding upon some of the glucose the rats digested down from the meals they ate. The entity within the body of a *Rattus norvegicus diabetica* that ate a large meal with a high carb count became very potent, while the entity within the body of a *Rattus norvegicus diabetica* that ate a small meal with a low carb count remained less potent. That's why Larry could never pinpoint where the presence was. Sometimes it seemed to be coming from a single location, that is, from a single rat that had eaten a large, high-carb meal, and at other times it seemed to be coming from all directions, that is, from many rats that had eaten large, high-carb meals.

After a while, even Larry stopped worrying about the presence because it never interfered with anything he wanted to accomplish using his own incredible powers. But something that bothered him greatly, something that even with his enlarged brain he could never figure out, was why the insulin injections had suddenly ended.

It made no sense. The entire purpose of the multimillion-dollar research project was to test Professor Tompkins's new insulin. The *Rattus norvegicus diabetica* had been specially bred for the project; the ALATs, LATs, LATGs, and vet techs had been specially trained for the project; and Dr. Schwartz's energy healers had been brought in to minister to the rats in a desperate effort to heal their hemorrhaging capillaries, prevent them from dying, and save the project.

So, what the hell? Larry thought. *What is going on? Who or what stopped the injections?* It was very perplexing to him that the very day after the injections stopped, every rat on his floor had been made part of a new experiment having nothing to do with diabetes. *Why let a good laboratory animal,* he thought, *go to waste?* The purpose of this new experiment was to test a new oral hair loss medicine that could be mixed in with the rats' food—no shots required.

R-Five suggested, "May ... maybe, the hu ... humans fi ... figur ... ou ..., uh, real ... realized that Pro ... Professor To ... Tompkins's in ... insulin is so effecti ..., uh, good that we don't nee ... need it an ... anymore."

Larry looked at him lovingly. R-Five's laborious manner forced Larry's enlarged brain to slow down and carefully consider each strained word. When he did that, he felt relaxed and happy. Although Larry could easily read the thoughts of his other cage-mates, he had difficulty reading R-Five's and sometimes suspected he could read them only when R-Five wanted him to.

Larry replied, "The humans didn't figure out anything. They think we need at least some of Professor Tompkins's insulin to survive, so believe me, they didn't just wake up one morning and end the whole project because they suddenly felt we didn't require it anymore."

Weeks passed, and Larry concentrated on nothing except how the research project suddenly had changed from testing lifesaving insulin to testing mere baldness medication in the space of a single day. He was desperate to understand and tried several times to increase his intelligence more by further enlarging his brain, but the process was slow and caused intense pain whenever he tried to exceed his daily limit.

He'd have possibly made himself ill, but he was saved by a growing biological urge that until now he'd been able to stave off with almost superhuma ... er, superrat effort. What he needed to do, and soon, was mate.

Chapter 8

Rats can breed when they reach three months of age, meaning Larry, now ten months old, had begun feeling urges long ago. They can also mate well into old age, which for them is three and a half years, with their maximum life span being about four. The oldest rat on record had lived seven years and four months, which by human standards is around one hundred sixty. Larry had already used his power to alter the physiology of any living thing so that he'd live well beyond that.

Since all his cage-mates were male, to find a breeding female, Larry would have to open his cage door. It would be a mass escape because he was bringing R-Five, One, Two, Three, and Four with him. But Larry could not open locked cage doors, or any doors, since his powers did not work on anything nonliving. There was no latch on the inside of his cage he could manipulate with his paws, only one on the outside. Figuring he'd have to get one of the techs to open it, he decided to suggest to Becky that she do it.

Strangely, thinking of Becky thrilled Larry. She was attractive with a great complexion, a good figure, and long auburn hair. His altered physiology, intelligence, and humanlike emotions often caused him to be aroused not only by the pheromones emanating from female rats, but also by those emanating from female humans.

Like Aubrey, Becky was deeply concerned about the well-being of her lab animals, and without being pushed much, she'd go out of her way and take risks to fulfill their needs. Moreover, since she was the manager of the lab rat colony, she'd be able to conceal any odd occurrences by creating or changing paperwork. She was the perfect candidate to help Larry escape.

For many hours, nonetheless, she fought like a wild woman to resist—a desperate attempt to remain in control of her thinking. Moments before Larry's suggestion sank in deep, she thought, *I can't believe what I'm about to do. I'll ruin the whole hair loss experiment and lose my job. What's happening to me?*

At six o'clock on a Friday evening, just as the weekend shift was taking over the care of the animals from the weekday shift, Becky did what in a million years she never believed she would do: she unhooked the latch on Larry's door and allowed him and his companions to rush out. She was so infuriated with herself that she barely noticed that Larry was walking haughtily erect on only his two hind legs, like a person, and not on all fours. She also didn't notice that the first thing Larry did was to hop atop a cabinet above where, on the wall, was a map of the entire floor. He carefully studied the map; it was apparent he could read the legend and every word. Larry's hormones had aroused him to the breaking point, so he studied the map for a long while to be certain he could find the females. But he probably needn't have done that; he could read their thoughts and, what's more, smell their pheromones.

He hopped down from the cabinet and, still erect on his hind legs, raced to the cages where the females were kept. Unable to restrain himself, he made a beeline to the cage where the most sexually potent one lived. Outside her cage, he used his front legs, which he'd altered to use like hands, to unhook the latch. He mounted her and within seconds felt release like he had when Moxus's aura combined with his, but better— much better!

In Larry's mind, an idea began to form, and as it did so, a mischievous grin, a Loki-like sneer, appeared on his lips. His mouth watered. His eyes glistened. *Seeing as this female was so good, what would one in the wild be like? never caged? untamed? raw and strong with nothing on her mind except prowling for sex?* He mounted the female again and went at her, brutally thrusting. She did not resist since, like Larry, she was way beyond her maturity date and had never mated before.

Satisfied, Larry relaxed, his four extremities entwined comfortably with hers. He made his mind reach out to sense the thoughts of *Rattus norvegicus diabetica 1–4* and R-Five. Not surprisingly, they had all mated too. But One, Two, and Four were already back in their cage. They'd forgotten to close their door, but an ALAT noticed that it was open and locked it shut behind them. Three had lingered for a while and was now locked out. He could not use his front legs like hands as Larry could and therefore was unable to unhook the latch. Aubrey walked by and let him in. She wondered how he'd gotten out in the first place. She was in a rush to finish some pressing tasks and did not notice that Larry and R-Five were missing.

Larry extracted himself from the grasp of the female and set about exploring the lab. Finding a discarded but only half-eaten sack of rat feed in a corner, he gorged himself. Then, dog-tired, he rested atop a shelf amid sealed insulin vials and plastic-wrapped syringes that, after Tompkins's PRT injections had suddenly stopped, lay unopened and unused. He shut his eyes, concentrated, and before collapsing into a deep sleep, cast his aura wide.

As often happened, try as he might, Larry had difficulty sensing R-Five. Had he really mated? Was he back in the cage with the others? If not, where was he? This time he could not sense R-Five's thoughts at all.

But for a fleeting moment he sensed the powerful presence he'd all but forgotten about.

PART II

BE KIND TO ALL CREATURES OF THE WORLD THAT THE HOLY ONE, BLESSED BE HE, CREATED

Chapter 9

Gary Schwartz and Simona Gupta had been part of the same seventh grade class in Tucson, and even then, their advanced aptitude for mathematics and science was apparent. In class, Gary's eyes always sparkled, his imagination constantly churning out visions of the incredible future discoveries he knew would be made. He sometimes asked his teachers questions like, "Can anyone around here tell me how many planets in our galaxy have life?" When he was told that no one was really sure, he said, "Well, why not? In 1961 Dr. Frank Drake figured out a formula to calculate that. The Drake formula estimates it's anywhere from one thousand to ten thousand, so even if his estimate is way off, I'm sure it's at least several hundred because there are a hundred billion stars in our galaxy and millions are like our sun with planets orbiting around them."

Coming from an eleven-year-old, well-spoken and persuasive answers like that astounded every adult. Gary could already think like a high school honor student, processing large numbers and computing probabilities in his very young mind.

Simona would often one-up him and say things that astonished her teachers too. One day, when the kids were being asked to recite the names of the planets in correct order, starting with Mercury, she blurted out, "Mrs. Johnson, I remember when Gary estimated there may be hundreds of planets in our galaxy that have life, but what I want to know is how many of those hundreds have advanced civilizations like us?"

The two often keyed off on each other like that and developed a deep affection for each other, which was long-lasting but never romantic. Not surprisingly, they both skipped a grade and finished junior high before they were thirteen. They'd have skipped two grades, but the principal thought, correctly, that neither of them would be mature enough, socially at least, to enter high school.

Gary's parents enrolled him at Tucson's Sonoran Science Academy, where he graduated as valedictorian, but Simona's father took advantage of a business opportunity in New York, moved the family there and enrolled her in the Bronx High School of Science. Despite the distance, the families stayed in touch. Over the years, after Gary earned PhD degrees in physics, chemistry, and astronomy, and Simona earned hers in biochemistry, anatomy, and zoology, they often worked on biotech projects together. They each gained international recognition for cutting-edge research testing pharmaceuticals on laboratory animals.

Gary had a friendly and outgoing personality, had a thick brownish beard, was a bit round in the middle, and had large brown eyes. He went on, incredibly, to obtain more degrees, these in general medicine, surgery, and psychiatry. What's more, after Moxus's hand-waving cured Larry and the other rats' bleeding blood vessels, Gary became an expert energy medicine practitioner himself. In 2007 he wrote a book titled *The Energy Healing Experiments*, which was groundbreaking and widely popular. He eventually became director of Development of Energy Healing for Canyon Ranch Resorts and also director of the Laboratory for Advances in Consciousness and Health at the University of Arizona.

Simona was far more reticent. Although born in the United States, she was of Indian descent and spoke fluent Hindi, which her parents often conversed in around the house, and Bengali, the language of the province they were from. She was tan-skinned, was just five foot one, and had very dark captivating eyes. Also, on the rare occasions when she removed her lab coat, she was surprisingly curvy, which together with her exotic good looks, always drew glances from her colleagues.

After Simona completed graduate studies at Harvard, her parents moved back to India. She remained in the United States and easily landed a position as a biochemistry professor at the University of Vermont. Her abilities were such that within five years she had won an international prize for isolating an enzyme that seemed to trigger diabetes, and within six years she was promoted, over several more senior colleagues, to be dean of the entire UVM Biomedical Research Department. Simona was obviously tenacious, and when she put her mind to something, it almost always got done. As her reputation grew, and along with it her income, she was able to visit her parents more frequently in Calcutta. The Indian scientific community was well aware of her credentials, and eventually she was invited to participate in biomedical research at Acharya Jagadish Chandra College. There, she would be able to conduct her cure-for-diabetes experiments using advanced primates, which was not yet illegal in India like it was back in the United States.

Simona spent the next many years traveling back and forth from her base at UVM, again, where she was dean of the Biomedical Research Department, and Acharya Jagadish Chandra College, where she regularly collaborated with her Indian colleagues testing pharmaceuticals on apes.

The only scientist associated with AJCC accorded more respect than she—and he only visited there infrequently as a sort of distinguished biomedical research honoree—was Professor Robert Tompkins. They were both members of Mensa thanks to their off-the-charts IQs—hers was 145, and his 160—and Simona admired him immensely. He was also the only man she had ever been physically attracted to.

Chapter 10

India: The Union Ministry of Environment and Forests
has banned the use of live animals in dissection and other
experiments in educational and research institutions. ...
Based on the Prevention of Cruelty to Animals Act, the
Union Ministry has issued guidelines to discontinue
experiments with live animals ... and instead use
alternatives like computer simulation.

What difference would it make that India had changed its laws to
prohibit using live animals in their country when PRT research was also
being done in the United States, where live animal testing was frowned
upon but not yet illegal? There, Tompkins could continue testing PRT to
his heart's content on rats, chimpanzees, and any other animals he wanted
to. Here was the problem though: almost all Tompkins's investors were
Indian based banks and the new law would prevent them from funding
live animal research anywhere.

So, when Gupta showed Tompkins the announcement in a Mumbai
newspaper, he immediately began estimating the amount of the bribes
he'd have to pay the Union Ministry bureaucrats for a waiver. No matter
what the price, he was certain his Indian investors would pony up because
the PRT research was too far along to walk away from and would almost
certainly earn them all huge profits. But his investors were sophisticated,
and explaining why he hadn't seen this coming would be difficult. They'd
already invested upward of sixty million dollars, and the necessary payoffs
would cost them several million more. They'd be angry, not just because
of the bribes, but also because the research was progressing much slower
than expected on account of the unusual side effect Tompkins hadn't let
them in on yet: his PRT morphed into a separate sentient being within
the body of each test animal injected with it. When they found that out,
they'd probably fire him on the spot and sue him for every last penny
they'd paid him.

If that happened, then Tompkins would hang himself from the nearest tree. He'd just turned seventy and all his life had struggled to support his family with relatively low-paying jobs teaching high school and university chemistry courses part time. He'd never earned more than sixty thousand dollars annually, without benefits. His ex-wife, a prekindergarten teacher, earned far less. She'd divorced him twenty-five years ago and taken their three teenage kids with her.

Until recently, when major investors had become interested in PRT, Tompkins could barely afford to pay rent on his studio apartment, maintenance on his decade-old car, or the premium for his health insurance.

Despite that, he could have had a passable social life because he was charming, fit, and tall and had thick gray-tinged hair. It wasn't infrequently that some of his attractive colleagues came onto him. But he never took them up on their offers. Not once. He simply had no interest. When he was fifty-one, he'd come down with adult-onset type 1 diabetes, which is rare—adult-onset diabetes is usually type 2—and ever since had remained almost totally impotent.

Even so, at UVM, when Simona first laid eyes on Tompkins, she fell madly in love, mostly because of his intellect, but also, in no small part, because she had convinced herself that whenever she removed her lab coat, her own physical charms would be irresistible and quickly arouse him.

*

After speaking with Gupta, whose fluency in Hindi and whose renown within the Indian biotech community enabled her to negotiate a reasonable bribe price, Tompkins made some calls. He phoned the vice president of India Overseas Bank, his largest investor, first. The two of them made small talk for a while until Tompkins explained the real purpose of his call *in code*. Both were aware that the Indian Security Services and the US National Security Agency, and maybe even the Chinese, might be listening in. The VP, unexpectedly, was resistant to coming up with the bribe money, so Tompkins forcefully reminded him of how much progress had been made, although it was slower than expected, in terms of developing his PRT at UVM and AJCC. The VP said, "What are you talking about? I don't know anything about any insulin research we funded at UVM. We're only funding insulin research at AJCC. The only thing we've got going on in the United States is baldness medicine research."

That reply brought Tompkins up short. There was just no way this VP could have forgotten the multimillions that Indian Overseas Bank had invested in the UVM insulin research. *Maybe,* he thought, *the guy is having a senior moment. A big one.* But Tompkins let it go.

They spoke awhile longer until finally the VP, realizing the bribes were necessary, said, "I'll see what I can do." Two hours later, the VP called back. He said, again in code, "Professor Tompkins, the arrangements have been made. What you need has been wired into an offshore account."

Over the next week, Tompkins contacted his other investors, and after similar conversations with each, they all agreed to pony up their share of the bribe money. Inexplicably, none of them remembered anything about the insulin research at UVM either. When Tompkins mentioned Dr. Gary Schwartz or Moxus, the names were totally unfamiliar to them. These guys had all invested multimillions in the UVM research and had always been intimately familiar with the names and credentials of everyone involved, so how could it be that now they were ignorant? Tompkins was perplexed and, to say the least, more than worried by this.

Suddenly, he sensed an invisible presence in the air hovering near him. The presence lingered, enveloping him, and for an uncomfortably long time, even he couldn't remember the details of the diabetes research at UVM. *Maybe,* he thought, *I'm having a senior moment like the VP from India Overseas Bank and my other investors.*

But he could clearly remember that he had often felt an aura emanating from cage 28, which was Larry's, One, Two Three, Four and R-Five's, just as Aubrey and Becky had. It was different from the presence he'd just felt but was at least as powerful.

Chapter 11

Larry awoke from his sleep atop the shelf in the UVM laboratory where he'd passed out. He was well rested and no longer bloated from the half sack of rat feed he'd devoured.

Free from his cage at last, Larry had no intention of returning to that little prison anytime soon. And that's exactly what it was to him: an unbearable, stifling, claustrophobia-causing prison cell lined with wood shavings to collect his and his cellmates' shit until it became such a stinking mess that an ALAT would come over and take it to the lab's cage-cleaning apparatus, where it would be lined with fresh wood shavings so they could start all over again and shit in that.

No, Larry was not going back, and he couldn't believe One, Two, Three, and Four had. *They are as stupid,* he thought, *as the humans. And speaking of the humans, who do they think they are kidding? The Three Rs? PETA? That might be enough for some dumb laboratory animals, but for a superior being like me? Give me a break.*

Larry prepared his mind for life on the outside, beyond the walls of the lab, because that's where he was going. His intelligence and abilities, still increasing daily, could handle anything out there. If only R-Five was with him to make his enlarged brain slow down once in a while, it'd be perfect.

Larry forced his aura to probe for miles in all directions and found he could connect with every living thing, all at the same time, in the entire city of Burlington—all one hundred thousand people; the millions of animals, including wild rodents, fish, and birds; and tens of millions of insects.

It was late autumn; the weather was turning cold. In a sewer two miles away, Larry sensed the presence of a thousand rats huddled together. The rats stank like the sewer and their fur was matted with each other's shit, and the sewer was mildewed and wet. Larry couldn't sense the wetness directly because water is inanimate, but he easily connected with the teensy auras of the billions of one-celled amoebas, paramecia, and other microbes swimming in it. Among the rats were hundreds of ravenous females. He longed for them.

To get outside and reach the sewer, Larry would have to try something he'd never done before. Scampering there, even on all fours, wouldn't do because if any of the techs were to spot him, he'd be caught and returned to his unbearable little cage. He wouldn't be able to stop them because, remember, it took several hours for any suggestions he implanted to sink in. He'd be back in his miserable cage with *Rattus norvegicus diabetica 1–4* before his suggestions took hold. And he wanted to leave now and not wait until he had control of the thoughts of every tech in the building. So, he concocted something new.

Larry decided he'd use his aura to transport himself, like Scotty transported Captain Kirk back and forth from the *Enterprise* countless millions of miles, to and from just about anywhere.

It worked. Larry was able to disassemble his body molecule by molecule, transfer those molecules to his aura, and then beam himself with pinpoint accuracy to the sewer, where he reassembled into his six-inch body.

The stench was incredible. His nostrils inhaled odors so nauseating that his stomach churned and even he, a fellow rat, vomited for several minutes. His puke drenched every rat around him, but they took no notice. Four of those rats were females. As Larry's stomach calmed, the pheromones radiating from them drove him wild. He selected one and mounted her, and she willingly relieved him.

Exhausted, Larry huddled with her and the others to shield himself from the dampness and cold. As he lay there, he thought, *Now what?* He pondered his next step for a long while.

Larry, intoxicated by the stink and savagery of his wild brothers and sisters, knew he was in his natural element. Here, outside and uncaged, rats were supreme. If not for the public exterminators, who regularly sprinkled poison in their hiding places, rats would have overrun Burlington long ago. Food, not lab food, but tons of rotting meat and putrid fish, was available for the taking from the humans' thousands of garbage cans and the city's dumps every day of the week. Female rats were everywhere, intentionally exciting the males with their overpowering pheromones. The males radiated pheromones too. Larry could have sex fifteen times a day if he wanted. The detestable humans had deprived him of that, but still, he couldn't deny that Aubrey, Becky, and most of the other techs had always been gentle and kind.

Larry lived in the sewer for weeks, surviving on scraps of the rotting meat and fish his fellow rats had hoarded there during the previous spring and summer. He stank like them, his hair grew filthy and matted with feces like theirs, and his claws and teeth became dagger-sharp like theirs. Larry became one of them, but with awesome intelligence and powers that continued to increase daily, very unlike them. These wild untamed rats, that is, *Rattus feras indomitus*, became his new companions, replacing his former cage-mates, *Rattus norvegicus diabetica 1–4* and R-Five.

Larry continued to ponder what he'd do next, and a plan began to form in his enlarged mind. His growing dislike for humans caused anger to course through him. His contempt for the human race was becoming uncontrollable. The reptilian portions of his brain were now almost as large as his cerebral cortex.

He selected five of the *Rattus feras indomitus* as his new inner circle and bathed them in his aura until their gray matter increased and they became intelligent and could speak.

But no one could replace R-Five, whom he loved and missed. Larry projected his aura all over the city scores of times but could never find him. That was the only thing keeping him from feeling invincible and complete.

Chapter 12

Inexplicably forgotten by all Tompkins's Indian investors that PRT testing had been in full swing in the United States, Simona Gupta doubled down on testing it on her diabetic apes at AJCC. Moreover, in secret from the Indian public, and known by only the heavily bribed Union Ministry Bureaucrats, she'd begun injecting PRT into human subjects even though several of the apes had become ill and some had died from it.

But Professor Tompkins's insulin experiment in the United States, and the cure-for-baldness experiment that suddenly replaced it, were not the only projects for which live animals had been used at the University of Vermont. Several years before either of those projects began, someone in UVM's School of Medicine borrowed from other schools the idea to intentionally injure pigs so surgeons could hone their skills trying to save them. The program, called Advanced Trauma Operative Management, first conceived in 2001 at the University of Connecticut, spread nationwide and was eventually offered at more than a hundred medical schools. Its purpose was to provide training for medics in treating soldiers who'd been grievously wounded in Iraq and Afghanistan.

At UVM, pigs' hearts, brains, livers, and other organs were deeply punctured, simulating bullet wounds, and the surgeons would operate using only the limited surgical tools and facilities that would be available on a battlefield. The animals often experienced horrific pain, equivalent to what can only be described as torture.

Here's a typical course listing:

Advanced Trauma Operative Case Management (ATOM)
Course Content

ATOM is an effective method of increasing surgical competence in the treatment of penetrating injuries to the chest and abdomen. The course consists of lectures followed by lab sessions in which instructors present

students with scenarios in which they must repair
simulated injuries using pigs to the following:

- bladder
- liver
- pancreas and duodenum
- spleen and diaphragm
- genitals
- heart and inferior vena cava.

A lab technician leaked what was going on at UVM to the media, and
when the news went public, the ASPCA, PETA, and every other animal
rights organization in the country went wild. Crowds of students, faculty
members, and Burlington residents rallied at protest demonstrations for
weeks.

Nevertheless, ATOM had many defenders. A lieutenant colonel who'd
been stationed at a field hospital near Baghdad asserted, "You can't simulate
the feel of real tissue using anything but a live organism. Pig hearts are the
closest you can get to human ones."

An assistant UVM dean said, "Pumping blood through human
cadavers doesn't reflect a real trauma situation. Difficult as it is to justify,
ATOM absolutely helps save lives."

Although ATOM was eventually shut down at most schools, including
UVM, thousands of pigs were maimed and operated on before it was
decided that a sufficient number of medics had been adequately trained.
After surgery, the pigs were kept alive for weeks so the surgeons could
monitor their recovery. They were then always put to death. As of 2018
ATOM w as still being offered at a handful of schools.

Larry took all this in. Tempered by his memories of the consistent
gentleness of most of the ALATs and LATs, and despite the ascending
dominance of the reptilian portion of his brain, he'd been able to keep
his growing hatred of humans in check. By reading Aubrey and Becky's
thoughts, he knew that their foremost concern was to minimize pain and
that the Three R's was their guiding light. But he'd been so focused on

his and his fellow rats' mistreatment, despite the Three Rs, including the imprisonment in cages and deprivation of sex, that he hadn't noticed the horrors other live animals were being subjected to. ATOM put him over the edge—way over! An anger so intense swept through him that it caused his blood pressure to skyrocket and his capillaries to start hemorrhaging again.

Temporarily, Larry returned to his cage. Doctor Schwartz brought in an energy healer, not Moxus, but a competent one nonetheless, to hand-wave over him. It worked, bringing his blood pressure back to normal. It did not reduce his rage.

Larry was about to hurl that rage at its intended target.

PART III

THE BLITZKRIEG ON
BURLINGTON

Chapter 13

Larry convened a meeting of his new inner circle, *Rattus feras indomitus 1–5*, and they assembled atop a low workbench in an abandoned shed near the sewer. One of the bulbs in an ancient light fixture overhead still worked, and Larry flicked the switch, having hopped on shelves to reach it. Although the members of his new circle were an innumerable number notches of intelligence beneath him, he'd boosted their intelligence enough so that they could understand him and, most importantly, obey his commands.

He said, "Have you finished contacting the colonies in the garbage dumps on the east side of the city, Feras 1?"

"I have, sir, and they can be ready at a moment's notice."

"And you, Feras 2, what is the status of the colonies in the housing projects along the canal?"

"They also will be ready, sir, and are awaiting your orders."

"And the Willow Park colonies—what of them, Feras 3?" Three was the female who had enticed Larry with her raging pheromones that first night and eagerly mated with him.

With effort, she managed to restrain herself from using the tip of her tongue to seductively wet her lips. She said: "They too are ready, Larry, and will do whatever you command."

At meetings, she was the only one allowed to address him as "Larry" rather than "sir," but otherwise she had to force herself to behave respectfully since Larry was the undisputed leader of the city's two million rats. Back in their nest, however, the screams that poured from her mouth, and Larry's, whenever they screwed were earsplitting. In fact, she'd become the dominant partner, always overwhelming him with her ferocious sexuality. In the three months since he'd arrived, she'd given him four litters, the care of whom Larry had assigned to other females so that nothing would prevent Three from succumbing to his advances. After mating, Larry, who's number was six—in fact, she called him Six during sex as another sign of intimacy—was always left totally spent.

Feras 4 was also female. Sex with her was almost as good and gave Larry some variety. Unlike Three, she was submissive and allowed herself to be dominated. She'd also given him several litters.

Four said, "The colonies on the north side are prepared, sir, and they will do whatever is necessary."

Larry had sent his inner circle to contact each colony in person, uh, that is, in rat, instead of communicating with them telepathically because he did not want to reveal the true extent of his powers to any *Rattus feras indomitus* outside his circle. Also, communicating telepathically by using his aura, he knew, would have the effect of increasing their intelligence and civilizing them somewhat, which was the last thing he wanted. His plans required that they remain unabatedly cruel and savage.

"What is your report, Feras 5?"

Larry had chosen *Rattus feras indomitus* 5 to be part of his new inner circle solely because he reminded him so much of R-Five. Needless to say, it was Larry who had given this particular rat the name Feras 5. He looked like R-Five; he spoke slowly and haltingly like R-Five; and his thoughts were sometimes difficult to read like R-Five's. But it was not the same. Larry only tolerated Feras 5's presence because, occasionally, the similarities to R-Five caused Larry's enlarged brain to slow down, making him feel happy and at ease. Without R-Five nearby, that rarely happened.

Feras 5 said, "The colon ... colonies in the se ... sewers do ... downtown are pre ... prepared, sir. We will fol ... follow your ord ... orders!"

*

Larry's rage against humans had been simmering below the surface, and when he learned about ATOM, it became full-blown hatred. He had not thought about the frequent kindnesses of Professor Tompkins, Aubrey, Becky or the other techs for weeks.

Even his inner circle, who despite their increased gray matter had become only two or three levels more civilized than their brother *Rattus feras indomitus* throughout the city, were unprepared for what Larry said next.

He announced, "The filthy humans have had their way too long. That must end because it is *we*, not they, who are superior. We breed faster, outnumber them twenty to one, and can survive on anything. We can live anywhere under any conditions, and our senses are stronger; we can smell and hear things a quarter of a mile away. And we're faster—much faster. Why should they live in mansions with comforts like heat and air-conditioning while we live in sewers? Why should they have delicious cooked food whenever they want it while all we have is their rotting leftovers? It's time for things to change. It's time for us to live in mansions and for them to live in sewers."

They were stunned. His inner circle also detested humans, but at most, they expected Larry's plan would be to organize the city's two million rats into a gargantuan foraging party that, with the spring weather approaching, could gather and stockpile enough food to get them comfortably through the next winter. But this? The humans would kill them all. *This was insane!*

But not to Larry. "What's the matter with you people—uh, rats? How many more of us do their exterminators have to poison before you'll rise up against them? Four hundred thousand? five hundred thousand? They slaughter three times that many of us in a year!"

After a long pause, *Rattus feras indomitus 1* said, "The colonies on the east side will follow you, sir. I will see to it." He was terrified, but more of Larry than of any retribution the humans might dole out.

Feras 3, the potent female, said, "The Willow Park colonies will follow you too. I will execute any deserters." She wasn't terrified but aroused.

Eventually, Feras 2, Feras 4, and even Feras 5 agreed to Larry's plan, although Feras 5 was much more reluctant than the others.

"We will reassemble in one week, when I will give you the details of our battle plan." And with that, Larry dismissed them.

But Three remained for a while and eagerly mated with him again.

Chapter 14

In truth, Larry had not thought through the details of a battle plan—or any plan for that matter. He'd been driven along thus far by deep anger, not logic, and simply hadn't thought about a detailed strategy. But with only a week to go until the next meeting, at which he'd have to give his generals, er, rats, meticulous orders, he got busy, and in his mind everything began falling into place.

He again considered whether to use his mental abilities to kill people, but he again decided not to because it would be too easy. He could just make them jump off roofs or something. He didn't want to use his mental powers on the city's two million rats much either because increasing their intelligence might civilize them more, and what he was really looking forward to was their viciously ripping the humans apart, bite by agonizing bite, wound by infected wound, until the humans—what a laugh that they called themselves that; they weren't human, they were animals—all lay writhing and died.

He could taste it. Larry could feel his teeth sinking deep into their flesh, even feeding on chunks of it. How could he have allowed them to mistreat him for so long? How could he have allowed them to use him like a stupid lab rat and stick him with needles for so long? And how could he have allowed them to imprison him and deny him sex for so long?

He would have sweet vengeance. He would have his generals order every *Rattus feras indomitus* in the city, all two million of them, to swarm from their hiding places en masse and assault every human they encountered. Then they'd retreat. They'd attack and retreat again and again until the humans, every filthy one of them, were grievously wounded.

The humans would retaliate. They'd send their exterminators to dump tons of poison into the rats' sewers, holes, and dens and kill hundreds of thousands. Every household would lay out dozens of traps and kill thousands more. But it would be a long war and Larry would order his generals to instruct each female to have as many litters as possible. In three months, those litters would mature and he'd have new soldiers to replace the casualties.

If necessary, he'd select generals from the city's five million mice, hundreds of thousands of squirrels and chipmunks, and hundreds of thousands of moles, gophers, and voles and instruct them to organize their hordes and join in the slaughter. The rotting flesh on the humans' corpses would not go to waste. The city's countless insects and birds, along with the rodents, would devour every delicious scrap.

Larry wrote everything down and drew maps. He planned in painstaking detail the routes his hordes would take—neighborhood by neighborhood, block by block, and house by house—to attack the humans. He'd spare no one, not children, not the homeless, not even PETA or ASPCA members, whose pretentious little show of concern for animals by running advertising campaigns to make everyone feel guilty so they'd adopt stray dogs sickened him. The only thing that mattered was that they were part of the disgusting human race and deserved to have their tongues torn from their arrogant mouths.

Joy coursed through Larry's veins. The visions of making people suffer dancing in his head gave him a euphoric high as though he was on crack. He paced, almost skipped along, in his drug-like ecstasy. After three days, filled with delightful thoughts of humans dying, he completed his battle plan.

*

Rattus feras indomitus 2, the general in charge of the colonies in the housing projects near the canal, walked in. "May I speak freely, sir?"

Larry eyed him. He didn't like his tone already. "Yes, go ahead. What is it?"

"Sir, I've been speaking with the other generals, and based on what you told us at our last meeting, we think you're planning an all-out war against people. Frankly, sir, we think the risks are unacceptably high."

Larry thought, *This pompous, stupid little rat. Who does he think he is talking to?* He controlled himself. "You're right, General. Our casualties will be high. But you and *Rattus feras indomitus 1, 3, 4,* and *5* aren't going to do the fighting. Only the hordes in the colonies, who can't talk or think and can barely wipe their own asses, will. So, who cares?"

Feras 2 fidgeted a long while, afraid to respond. Finally, he said, "Sir, I have scores of children in the colonies who can't speak or think, but I don't want them to die needlessly. And forgive me, sir, but you have hundreds more children than I do. Everyone knows you've had dozens of litters with Feras 3, Feras 4, and other females. Do you really want most of them to die when the humans counterattack?"

Despite his growing rage, which he could barely contain, Larry knew that Two had a point. "How do the other generals feel? Did you really speak with them, or did you just come in here on your own?"

"No, sir. I spoke with them at length, and they agree with me."

"Well, General, what about the females? Did you speak with Three and Four?"

"I did, sir, but I want to be completely honest and accurate. When I told them my concerns, Four just nodded at me with a worried look in her eyes. Three, however, rushed to check on her litters, whom you assigned other females to care for. She's with them now and says she won't leave them until she's sure they're safe."

That gave Larry something to think about. Not because he was worried about his children, but because he might have to do without sex with Three for a while.

"Thank you for your honesty, General. Do you have anything else to say?"

"No, sir, I think I've made my point, and I hope you will consider it."

"Feras 2," Larry replied, "I will consider everything you've said, but tell the others this: my orders will be followed to a T without question. This is not a democracy. You all will obey them or hang."

Crushed, Feras 2 gathered himself and, scampering on all fours, left. As he did so, he passed *Rattus feras indomitus 5*, who was on his way in.

It was uncanny how much Feras 5 reminded Larry of his old friend R-Five. Sometimes he thought Feras 5 was R-Five in disguise. But the moment Feras 5 spoke, the resemblance vanished. "I wa ... want you to sto ... stop this insa ... insanity. You have no r ... right to fo ... force us to ma ... march to our deaths bec ... because you li ... lived in a ca ... cage for a while."

R-Five would never have spoken to Larry like that. "Watch yourself, Five. You're on the brink of insubordination. I won't tolerate it."

"Larr ..., uh, sir. I wish to be re ... relieved of com ... command. If you plan to ord ... order us to kill the hum ... mans, I wi ... will not ob ... obey."

"You're relieved!" Larry shot back. "That's exactly what I'm planning. If you refuse, you'll be charged with treason then tried, convicted, and hanged."

Five, with no fear of Larry at all, said, "Wh ... who the he ... hell made you ki ... king? I reme ... remember that you ju ... just sho ... showed up one d ... day and to ... took over."

Larry no longer found Feras 5's slow and halting manner of speech endearing. "I'm placing you under house arrest. If you attempt to leave your place in the sewer, you'll be executed on the spot. You've misjudged me, Five. I will not kill just the humans but anyone who sympathizes with them. Return to the stinking sewer where you belong. Soon you'll be joined there by whatever humans survive."

At least Larry knew for certain where his inner circle stood. Feras 5 and the females Three and Four would definitely not obey him. Larry did not want to use his aura to enlarge their brains further so he could more strongly influence their thoughts because it would further civilize them. That might make them even more uncooperative and drive them to spread dissension among the ranks. For now, house arrest for all three would do.

Larry felt he could count on One and Two. He'd selected them for his inner circle and had designated them his top generals in the first place because he knew they'd be the most reliable. He summoned them.

"Gentlemen, we need three new generals. Feras 3, Feras 4, and Feras 5 have been relieved of command. Make the arrangements. Have them ready to participate in our next meeting. We'll delay it a few days so you'll have time to bring them up to speed."

But before they could respond, Feras 3 rushed in, hysterical. Her entire body was trembling, and tears poured from her tiny eyes. She had difficulty breathing, and a crystallized blue substance was matted in her fur. She could barely speak and was shaking uncontrollably. Her nose dripping blood, she gasped:

"The humans have attacked. They're using difethialone and indandione poisons. Larry, half our children are dead!"

Chapter 15

Larry was so shocked that he forgot about putting anyone other than Feras 5 under arrest. The detestable humans had launched a lethal preemptive strike, but how—*how*—could they have known what he was planning? Rage consumed him, rage beyond anything he'd ever felt, and he cast his aura wildly toward Burlington's Department of Rodent Control, angrily searching for its manager.

When he found him, a man named Tom Garret, he was calmly sitting at his desk receiving reports from his field chiefs. Larry read his thoughts while intentionally inflicting a piercing pain. That caused Garret to rub his temples, thinking, *Jesus, one of my migraines is coming on.*

It wasn't a preemptive strike, Larry learned, just a regular but rescheduled one, and the humans were exterminating with new, deadly, effective second-generation poisons, not the first-generation poisons they usually used.

Difethialone and indandione kill by bringing on massive internal hemorrhaging, bleeding mouths and nasal passages, shortness of breath, extreme shock, and even bleeding eyes. The victims die in intense, excruciating agony. It was amazing Feras 3 was alive.

Larry immediately imprinted suggestions into Garret's and his field chiefs' minds to stop using the new poisons and revert to the old ones. It took twenty-four hours before the suggestions sank in, and by then Larry's rat army had been reduced by two hundred fifty thousand.

When the old poisons were used, they always killed far fewer, but just enough to keep the rat population at around the usual two million. Larry could have stopped Garret from using any poisons, but if he had done that, then their population would have exponentially multiplied to four million at least and they'd be able to slaughter all the humans in a day. Larry didn't want that. Now, more than ever, he wanted all of Burlington's people to suffer for a long time. He wanted the survivors of the first attack to be terrified beyond imagining as they saw their neighbors, friends, and family members dying around them. The rats would attack every day, and those humans who survived each attack would be more and more terrified, awaiting their turn to die.

Larry glared at Three angrily. "Our children?" he shouted. "How could you have allowed half of them to be slaughtered? I told you to herd them into the deepest end of the sewer."

"I did!" Three shouted back. "But the ones whom the new poisons killed were our youngest and so small that just two or three crystals of difethialone was a lethal dose. I tried to protect them, Larry. I'm half dead myself. Look at me."

"What about my other children? Where's Feras 4?"

"Half your children with her are also dead. And, Larry, she's dead too."

For a moment, he lost it, but he quickly recovered. His interest in having children never had anything to do with being a good parent. His motive, aside from sex, was to create as many strong young soldiers as possible to help replace whatever casualties his two-million-strong army suffered in the war against humans.

Replacements were what Larry needed now. He leered at Feras 3, ignoring her bleeding mouth and nose. He advanced at her, lasciviously licking his lips, and for the first time since he'd arrived in the sewer, she resisted instead of spreading her legs. As he began to mount her, she recoiled in horror and fought with all her strength, but he overpowered her and raped her again and again. He left Three bleeding and in even more pain than from the difethialone. She detested him but could do nothing. When she lunged at his throat with her bare claws, he pierced her mind painfully with his aura and easily held her off. With the last of her ebbing strength, she clawed at him again, but it was futile.

Neither Feras 4—obviously, because the poisons had killed her—nor Feras 5, who was under house arrest, had been present when the rape was happening. One and Two, however, witnessed the whole thing and were now just inches from Three's bleeding body, which lay crumpled at Larry's feet.

"Let this be a lesson to anyone who dares challenge my orders again. Is that absolutely clear to you gentlemen?"

Feras 2, who just a day ago had tried to persuade Larry not to launch his insane war, immediately nodded.

But Feras 1, the most loyal of his generals, with his eyes glistening, said, "I can't wait to begin, sir. I've already selected three officers to replace Three, Four, and Feras 5, and their loyalty is beyond question.

"For your sake, General, let us hope so."

For a long while, despite his enthusiasm, pure fear coursed through One's tiny body.

PART IV

ACHARYA JAGADISH
CHANDRA COLLEGE

Chapter 16

At AJCC, another of Gupta's live animals died. This time it was a twelve-year-old chimpanzee very weak from diabetes, but it wasn't his type 1; it was a fatal overdose of the ape PRT that she and Tompkins were testing that killed him. Fortunately, she was so well respected by the Union Ministry of Environment bureaucrats, and they'd been so well bribed, that they did nothing about it. However, the negligent tech who had administered the overdose was quietly let go and was required to sign a nondisclosure agreement in exchange for a generous severance package.

Nevertheless, the incident caused Gupta and many on her staff to do some soul-searching. One evening, in her modest residence on the AJCC campus, she was surfing the web and came across a debate page. The topic was live animal testing, and the moderator had kicked off the discussion this way:

"There is a raging controversy afoot between those who think lab animal research is inhumane cruelty and those who insist it is an unfortunate necessity to find new cures for illnesses and injuries. The controversy has intensified as biomedical research has accelerated and animal rights organizations have become better funded. Both sides may by be right!"

Following are some arguments posted by members of the public online either in favor of or against using live animals for research:

We're Talking Human Lives, People

Say a loved one has been diagnosed with a once fatal disease; it may be because of animal research that medicine can help them live. If I had to choose between the life of a dog and the life of my brother, child, niece, or nephew, or any other person I knew, I would pick the person.

What Have We Become?

People, *open your eyes*. Just because we are a "superior" species does not give us the right to harm helpless, defenseless, innocent animals. If we are so superior, then why have we failed to find another way to test? There is no excuse, absolutely no excuse, to harm any living thing, even if it is for the benefit of humans. Think about yourselves in that position: hopeless, scared, sad. Really think about it. What kind of a life is that? It's a life that no innocent living creature should have to go through. *Wake up* and realize that humans are losing their sensitivity, their humaneness.

If There Are No Better Alternatives, Animals Should Be Used for Research

Animal testing is not always ideal, but it remains necessary for research. While it is important to consider the well-being of animals when conducting such research, we must also recognize the potential knowledge, developments, and discoveries that can be gained. Since such research can lead to new products and medicines that have the potential to improve and save the lives of both humans and animals, it is justified.

Gary Schwartz walked in. There was no knock because Simona was eagerly expecting him and had left the door open. She rose from her desk, and they wildly embraced. He and Simona were still dear friends, and he visited her in India once every year. They also saw each other almost monthly back in the States, either at UVM or the University of Arizona in Tucson, the latter being where Gary lived, or at biomedical research conventions around the country.

Although Gary was not involved in the ongoing PRT research, he and Simona continued to collaborate on the use of energy medicine to reduce stress in lab animals and on several other projects.

They always looked forward to seeing each other because, like when they were kids, they could fool around, giggle and joke, and just enjoy being together. Friends made in childhood are the best because no matter how many degrees or riches they earn later in life, who they really are remains etched forever into each other's hearts.

Gary sat down next to Simona and started watching the online debate with her:

How Dare Us!

How can we test harmful chemicals on innocent animals and interfere with and possibly destroy their lives? I realize some people love the human race and want us not to suffer. Making others suffer is not the way. This cruel way of testing cosmetics and sometimes finding new medicines should be stopped. Why don't we do the testing on other humans?

Stop Taking Medicine, People Who Are Against This

People who are against treatment of animals for medical purposes, kindly stop taking medicines or any kind of vaccine. As we all have advanced to the modern era from the Stone Age, this transformation has seen many advancements that have made not only humans', but also animals', lives better.

Would You Do Those Things To A Human?

Animals shouldn't be used for testing. It is totally unfair to the animal being tested. They don't have a choice, or a voice of their own to say no or defend themselves. I know it's to make sure products are safe for humans, but animals think and feel just as much as we do.

Animals Should Be Used For Research

Animal testing was one of the main starting points for the invention of penicillin. Drug testing is an important and long process. In a world that is so dependent on the reliability and advancements of medicine, it would be strange not to test new methods in some way. Would you rather a possibly beneficial drug be tested on humans before animals?

Gary and Simona had considered the same arguments over and over during their careers: *Intentional cruelty or infliction of pain to animals is a sin, but ...*

As they sat close to one another on a small couch watching, they discussed the online arguments and even posted a few themselves. Occasionally, Simona's bare thigh brushed lightly against Gary's, but neither took notice. They were true childhood buddies and always would be. Their relationship just didn't include any physical intimacy.

Humans Should Be Wiped Out Of Existence

Humans just test on animals because of the curiosity of it. There is no need to study and kill the animals. Humans should be tested on instead of animals because the results would be more defined. Humans are already used for testing by the FDA. About 92 percent of drugs that work on animals are dangerous to humans. If humans never existed, the world would be a better place. No global warming, animal abuse, or any of the other bad things you can name.

Animal Testing Has Significantly Improved Human Welfare

Experience has shown what invaluable advances can be made in medicine by experimenting on animals, and live animals are the most reliable subjects for testing medicines and other products for toxicity. In many countries, all prescription drugs must be tested on animals before they are allowed onto the market. To ban animal experiments would be to paralyze modern medicine, to perpetuate human suffering, and to endanger human health by allowing products such as insecticides onto the market before testing them for toxicity.

This Is Madness

Animals are being treated horribly, people! We need to stop this. I believe we should use prisoners who will never get out of prison instead of animals. And I do get that if some of your family members are in prison forever, you might not want to consider this. But if they are sentenced to life or ninety-nine years, there is no chance for them. They would be good test subjects, I would think.

Face It, People Against Testing: Most Animals Are Crueler Than We Are

In the wild, dear people, animals are often brutally vicious. Hyenas and grizzly bears, for example, will take down prey and begin feeding while it's still alive. Male lions, elephant seals, and wolves, and the males of dozens of other species, will fight to the death to win the favor of females during mating season. And the females aren't innocent; they approve. When's the last time you heard of a shark, crocodile, or poisonous snake sparing the life of an innocent child? Never! Rat packs inflict bites, not just on humans, but also on each other, which spreads disease worldwide. Even chimpanzees sometimes viciously attack monkeys and other chimps and cannibalize them. And you've all heard about Charla Nash, whose face was ripped off in 2009 by her friend's pet chimp. It tore off her nose, ears, and lips, and left her permanently blind from infection. That's the natural order of things, animal lovers. In my opinion, we should definitely use animals for medical testing because the cures discovered will improve our and our loved ones' survival rate and that of animals too.

Simona recognized the grammar and cadence of that last comment and realized it had been posted by the ALAT who'd accidentally overdosed her chimpanzee.

Gary said, "I agree with that guy. He is absolutely right."

It was an intelligent comment but would be hated by PETA types. And the savagery of the wild animals the poster had mentioned definitely didn't apply to the chimpanzee Tompkins's insulin had killed.

Still distraught by the chimp's death, Simona immediately decided to temporarily stop all tests of the PRT on apes, but she was worried. *Will Tompkins and I ever be able to reformulate it so that human testing will be safe? And how much longer will our investors hang in before they fold and cut off funding?*

Chapter 17

It took two days for Three to awake from her coma. The difethialone and rape hadn't killed her, but if she didn't drink and eat soon, then thirst or starvation would. She gathered herself and drank from a fetid puddle, then crawled slowly toward the deep end of the sewer, where her surviving children were being tended to. Before rushing to them, she fed on a few barely edible slivers, even for rats, of moldy putrefying meat.

She sensed something. At first, she thought it was Larry casting his aura to cause pain again. But, although very powerful, it was different from the aura and emanating from nearby. For a moment she thought she recognized the slow and halting speech pattern of Feras 5, but as suddenly as it had come, it vanished. It hadn't been painful, but peaceful.

Revived from the scraps, Three found the few of her children who had survived and examined each of them from head to toe. Some of their noses and mouths were still bleeding but otherwise they seemed fine. The females Larry had selected to care for them had excavated four feet of muck from the sewer's deep end and then dragged Three's still alive offspring there to shield them from the next attack. By herself, Three excavated another foot and dragged them deeper.

Satisfied they were safe for the time being, she turned her attention to laying to rest the bodies of her many children who had succumbed to the poisons. Strangely, they were no longer where she'd seen them die before she slipped into a coma two days ago. For a quarter hour, Three searched the passageways the colony had burrowed, some of them fifteen yards long, into the thick sewer sludge. As she rounded a turn in one of the longest of these passageways, ahead of her was a scene that would make Charles Manson's worst nightmare look serene. She'd located scores of the decaying bodies of her kids strewn among rancid piles of fish and meat that the rat colony had stored there. In disbelief, she saw ten adults cannibalizing her babies. She charged at them in a wild rage in a desperate attempt to make them stop. They easily shrugged her off as Larry had and continued feeding.

Three collapsed in a corner and forced herself into an unthinking deep sleep. It was the only thing she could think to do to shut off the nightmarish scene she had come upon. In an hour she awoke, but she lay there motionless for an hour more, afraid to open her eyes.

Rattus feras indomitus 5 was standing over her. "P ... please do not tr ... try to get up yet, Three. You ... you've be ... been thr ... through too m ... much."

"Am I in hell or actually still alive somehow?" She gasped.

"Yo ... you're ve ... very much al ... alive and, I hope, st ... still sane eno ... enough to help me."

"Help you with *what*?" She glanced to her right, and alongside her children's mangled bodies was the lifeless body of one of the rats who'd cannibalized them, a hideous looking male with scraps of one of her baby's flesh still protruding from its mouth.

"Did you kill that monster, Feras 5?" she asked.

"I w ... was abo ... about to ask you the sa ... same th ... thing. The bo ... body was th ... there when I wa ... walked by and saw you l ... lying here."

"Then who killed him?

"You have many symp ... sympathizers, Three. When word sp ... spread ab ... about what Larry had d ... done to you, ma ... many in the colo ... colonies were an ... angered. When so ... some of your sympa ... uh, friends saw what th ... that rat was fe ... feeding on, th ... they m ... must have ki ... killed him."

Three trembled, unable to push the image of her kids' half-eaten bodies from her mind. Finally, she asked, "Help you with what?"

"We m ... must stop Larry. The hu ... humans have even more pow ... powerful poisons. They have third-gen ... gener ... generation p ... poisons and will use them, even though those p ... poisons, once re ... released, will kill m ... many of the hu ... humans too."

"Are you crazy talking like that? Larry may be reading our thoughts right now."

"I kn ... know, b ... but he has diff ... difficu ... difficulty re ... reading mine. For some rea ... reason, he c ... can't g ... get a fix on me."

"What about me, Five? He'll rape me and torture me again."

"No, Three. Wh ... when yo ... you're n ... near me, I don ... don't th ... think he can read yo ... your thoughts ei ... either. You're prot ... protected too."

But as near as Feras 5 was to her, she sensed nothing. No emanations, no presence, nada. The emanations she'd momentarily felt when she awoke had to have come from Feras 5. She was sure they had, but now she sensed absolutely nothing at all.

Chapter 18

In the abandoned shed near the sewer, Larry convened the long-delayed second meeting of his inner circle. *Rattus feras indomitus 1* and *2* sat on either side of him. The three new officers, Feras 6, Feras 7, and Feras 8, sat opposite.

Larry disliked Seven the moment he laid eyes on him. A feisty little son of a bitch, he dared to speak before Larry had given him permission. Seven, as well as Six and Eight, were not as intelligent as One and Two because Larry had begun enlarging their brains only days ago, but that was no excuse.

"Shut your mouth!" Larry shouted. "And don't open it again till you're told to." One fidgeted uncomfortably. He had chosen Seven, along with Six and Eight, and Larry would hold him accountable.

Larry spoke: "We will concentrate our first attack in the city's tight, one-square-mile downtown during the evening rush hour. The humans will be tired after working all day and won't know what hit them. I want all the colonies to converge there at exactly five o'clock one week from now. As the humans head toward bus and train stops or their cars, we'll inflict hundreds of bites on each of them, and thousands will probably die from shock in the first wave. No one is to be spared. In fact, I want you to go after the sickest and weakest first, which will guarantee numerous instant kills, and spread terror among the rest. Their corpses are to be ripped apart and fed upon on the spot. How many of our females will have to stay behind to tend to our litters?"

"No more than thirty thousand, sir," One said. "That will be enough to care for our four hundred sixty thousand very young. The rest of us, including all aged three months or older, will join in the assault. We'll be one million five hundred thousand strong."

Two chimed in with, "The humans downtown will number eighty thousand at most. The rest work elsewhere, are unemployed, or will be home tending *their* young."

Turning to Seven, Larry said, "You may speak now. Do you have anything intelligent to add?"

"I do, sir. As you know, I've taken over command of the Willow Park colonies from Feras 3 and will personally lead them into battle."

Feras 3. Larry relished her name, recalling her pheromones. His genitals swelled.

"Your enthusiasm is commendable, Seven, but getting yourself swatted by a human and injured or maybe killed is not what you're here for." The little prick. Larry detested him more with each passing second. "The humans are gigantic and physically strong. They're five hundred times heavier than us. None of you will get near them. I will say this once: your job is to make sure your troops do the killing, not you. I want all of you uninjured so you can lead each subsequent attack. Is that clear?"

"It is, sir. I apologize for getting carried away."

Larry looked angrily toward One. *Where did Feras 1 find this moron?* Turning to Two, he asked, "Have you located Feras 5 yet?"

Trembling because he knew what Larry's reaction would be, One replied, "I've sent one hundred of my best troops to look for him, sir, but he's vanished."

Larry let that sink in. He cast his aura far and wide but sensed nothing. He'd always had difficulty sensing Five's thoughts, but usually there was at least something.

Two said, "And, sir, forgive me, we can't find Three either. She's vanished too."

Larry thought, *Maybe Three and Five are dead.* When he'd last seen Three, she was bleeding from every orifice. Maybe the rats who'd devoured their children's bodies had also devoured hers? Maybe they'd devoured the traitor Five's body too?

But he knew that wasn't true. More likely, they were in hiding, plotting to undermine his battle plan. But why would they go to such great lengths to avoid doing what rats naturally did—swarm, bite, eat flesh, and inflict pain? It didn't make sense. Why couldn't the hundred rats Feras 2 had sent find them? And why couldn't Larry's aura pick up any of their thoughts? Not a single one? Where the hell were they?

It dawned on him that they couldn't be doing this alone. Someone was helping them. His inability to sense Feras 5's thoughts reminded him of the difficulty he'd always had sensing his old friend R-Five's. Aside from the probable incompetence of the moron Seven on the battlefield, Larry now had something to worry about he hadn't bargained for.

Chapter 19

Although he'd initially firmly decided against it, more than once Larry considered changing his mind and using his aura to slaughter the humans. It would be better than relying on his new generals, who would probably get themselves killed in the first assault. He was none too happy with One and Two either, since One had chosen the new generals and Two had gone along with it. With whatever sanity remained in him, however, Larry knew that just killing people with his aura wouldn't be satisfying. It would be too quick. What he wanted, above all else, was to see them writhing in torment.

It had been almost four months since Moxus had ministered to him and their combined auras had grown frighteningly powerful. Larry decided to test the aura's true strength and cast it throughout the city again. As before, he easily connected with the one hundred thousand people; hundreds of thousands of mammals, birds, amphibians, and reptiles; millions of insects; and billions of microbes. The only living things he couldn't connect with were Feras 3, Feras 5, and above all R-Five, whom he still loved and missed.

Concentrating intently, he forced his energy field beyond the city's borders and throughout the entire state. That too was easy, and he connected effortlessly with every living thing under every log and rock, on every hill, and in every tree and home.

Concentrating more, he was able to use his aura to read the thoughts of every living thing all at the same time everywhere in the United States. As the adage goes, "Absolute power corrupts absolutely," and Larry was about to prove it. He gathered himself and, with a gargantuan burst of energy, found he could project his aura throughout the world. For hours, he took sheer megalomaniacal delight in his ability to explore thousands of cities on every continent. His ego soared. He was able to use his enlarged mind to probe, absorb, and even taste new sights and sensations he had never imagined existed.

On a whim, he focused his aura on Calcutta and knew at once that parts of it were the most rat-infested places on the planet. Like he'd done to escape his cage, Larry disassembled his body molecule by molecule, transferred the molecules to his aura, and then beamed himself to Calcutta's slums, where he reassembled into his six-inch body. The slums' garbage-strewn streets teemed with rats that outnumbered the two million rats in his home city by a factor of a hundred. There were nearly a quarter billion. In the sewers, there weren't just hundreds of sexually ravenous females, there were hundreds of thousands. Larry didn't have to mount them; three immediately overpowered and mounted him one after the other. There was one in particular, larger and stronger than Larry, who within fifteen minutes mated four times with him until at last she was satisfied.

She told him, with the squeaks and snarls primitive rats used to converse, that her name was Glerichatuniviyuak (translated as Glenda). Other than signaling that she wanted sex or food, her name was the most sophisticated idea she could communicate. She was far more primitive than Three, and she thrilled Larry tremendously. He was thrilled by all the city's primitive rats and probed all their minds. Like Glenda, they were incapable of what one would call thought. Identifying themselves with names, not human-sounding names but rat ones, was the limit of their thinking ability.

Using his aura, Larry explored every nook and corner of Calcutta and discovered that even there, amid the squalor, there were many upscale, civilized places including top-rated universities. One of them was Acharya Jagadish Chandra College (AJCC), named after the road it was located on. It had a world-renowned biomedical research department with a cutting-edge animal lab, and three of its professors, including Gupta, were Nobel Prize winners.

On foot, Larry explored the lab, in whose cages were hundreds of Calcutta's rats. These were not specially bred *Rattus norvegicus diabetica* rats but *Rattus feras indomitus* (wild rats), being used in an experiment Larry knew well. He didn't need his aura to know what substance was being tested on them, because he could smell it. They were being injected with the same thing Larry had been injected with thousands of times. He could barely believe it, but the *Rattus feras indomitus* were being injected with PRT.

What Larry saw next, he couldn't accept. He thought his mind was playing tricks on him, and he nearly fainted, as heading toward a rack of the cages, with several ALATs in tow, was Ron Carter. And walking beside him as if it was the most natural thing in the world was Professor Robert Tompkins.

Shocked to see them, Larry was also shocked by the experiment they were performing. He knew that type 1 diabetes occurred in only 4 percent of wild rats. The rats in the cages had been collected randomly from outside, so only 4 percent of the rats in these cages had type 1 and 96 percent did not. That huge majority had plenty of natural insulin circulating in their bloodstreams, and for them PRT injections just weren't necessary.

Seeing Tompkins, and Carter, had so startled Larry that for several minutes he couldn't read their thoughts. He literally fell off the table he was standing on. Gathering himself, he listened:

"You were saying, Carter?"

"Yes, Professor, I think the results so far have been as expected."

"Well, has your team here made any progress in controlling the problem with my self-adjusting insulin?"

"No, sir. We've been injecting the smallest doses of your insulin possible to keep the Calcutta rats' type 1 diabetes under control, but it still becomes sentient and develops a consciousness."

"Have you blended in the exact amount of nonadjusting regular insulin as I instructed you to do? It should have worked. Let me look at the formula you've been using."

Carter handed him some paperwork with detailed chemical equations. Tompkins studied them carefully.

"Yes, and as you wanted, Professor Gupta has checked and rechecked all my ingredients and procedures. When we eliminate your insulin's capacity to, uh, think by diluting it too much, it also loses its capacity to self-adjust."

Tompkins was at an impasse. Short of pancreatic cell implants into diabetic patients, PRT was the closest thing to a cure that had ever been developed. Pfizer Pharmaceuticals had offered him a billion dollars for the patent if it proved effective on humans, and there was even talk of his getting a percentage of the profits when it went to market. But that a sentient living being arose within the body of each rat the PRT was injected into was an insane and dangerous side effect. The reason that happened, Tompkins suspected, was not because of his PRT alone, but its interaction with the specific disease: *type 1 diabetes*, not just any disease like leukemia or hemophilia. He wanted incontrovertible proof that he was right.

He ordered Carter to induce comas in twenty of the diabetic rats and film them by using cameras that could photograph the auras emitted by all living things. These natural auras were like Larry's was before it combined with Moxus's and gave him incredible powers.

At first, Carter refused because he thought induced comas would be life-threatening and, like Aubrey and Becky, he was guided by the Three Rs, which above all else prohibited causing lab animals unnecessary pain. But Tompkins insisted, so reluctantly, Carter agreed and induced the comas. What the cameras recorded was startling.

Whenever these cameras had previously been used, they always recorded weak auras emanating from animals' bodies that on film looked like very faint halos. The cameras recorded weak auras emanating from plants too. It is these auras that energy healers are able to interact with, and also why some mystic types believe they can talk to their house plants and the plants can respond. But the auras the cameras recorded surrounding the bodies of the diabetic rats that had been injected at AJCC were anything but weak. They were dark and solid and extended outward from the rats' bodies to the edges of the film. The auras were so dark that they could barely be distinguished from the rats' corporeal bodies in the centers of the pictures.

Tompkins had instructed Carter to inject both the diabetic rats and a group of nondiabetic leukemia-afflicted rats with his self-adjusting insulin so he could see, by comparing what the cameras recorded, if the bodies of the leukemic rats would emanate dark solid auras too. They didn't—just the weak auras around living things the cameras always recorded. But why?

He realized that he'd been right: it was the interaction of his PRT with the specific disease, type 1 diabetes, that caused the dark solid auras, but this was the same interaction that turned PRT into a separate, sentient being within the body of each rat injected with it. That's why it could self-adjust on its own, almost as if it could think by itself.

Such an insane side effect was frightening, and unless he could eliminate it, Tompkins knew that PRT could never be injected into type 1 diabetic *humans* to create sentient living beings within their bodies too. He became desperate because he saw the one billion dollars Pfizer had promised him slipping away. Pfizer wouldn't pay him a cent, nor would any other pharmaceutical company.

The possibility of losing the one billion drove Tompkins crazy, until the idea crossed his mind that what he'd discovered might be much more valuable than even a cure for diabetes. He'd been so fixated on discovering a cure that he'd overlooked for a while that he'd actually created life. Scientists had been trying to do so for decades, but the farthest they'd gotten was to grow clones of sheep from cells harvested from sheep and stored in test tubes. That was pretty far, but it was nothing compared to what he'd come upon.

Tompkins realized there was no longer any point in concealing what his insulin could do from the Pfizer executives. He'd call them and explain what he'd discovered and show them the dark solid auras on the films. He'd explain that somehow his insulin could think and that's why it could self-adjust. They'd go wild thinking about the possibilities. If he and Gupta could tweak the PRT formula a bit, so it would interact with any disease, not just type I diabetes, who knew what such insulin could do for Parkinson's, Alzheimer's, dementia, and brain injuries? The Pfizer execs would imagine, not tens of billions in profits, but tens of trillions, and give him unlimited research money. They'd reach for their checkbooks and pay him, not one billion for his patent, but several billion.

Intense pain suddenly pierced his mind. Tompkins staggered, fell back against a wall, and screamed. Before anyone saw him and rushed to help, the professor collapsed to the floor facedown. Just before losing consciousness, he saw a furry six-inch shape scamper away. It was different from Calcutta's rats. It was more like a *Rattus norvegicus diabetica* from UVM.

It was *Rattus norvegicus diabetica 6*: Larry!

PART V

OTHER WORLDS

Chapter 20

If Tompkins's mind had been pierced just a bit more forcefully, he'd have died, but what Larry did accomplish, bursting blood vessels in his head, was enough. Tompkins was hospitalized for three weeks, and when he was discharged, after two sessions of laser surgery to cauterize bleeding brain tissue, he still couldn't speak without slurring.

Causing Tompkins pain had felt great, but Larry was disgruntled about one thing. He had intended to kill Tompkins right then and there, and that he hadn't been able to scared him. An invisible force had stopped his aura from reaching maximum strength, so powerful he couldn't overcome it.

Larry reached the conclusion that the force was the presence he had worried could do things even he couldn't achieve. So, to prove to himself he was still the most awesomely powerful thing in the universe, he attempted something so incredible that there'd be no doubt. He cast his aura beyond Earth and, by traveling at light speed, succeeded in reaching other planets. Not satisfied with reaching just Venus, Mars, and the other planets in our solar system, he discovered how to reach planets in distant galaxies. Here's how he did it:

He started by casting his aura toward the Magellanic Clouds, the galaxies nearest to ours, at the speed of light, one hundred eighty-six thousand miles per second, but realized that even going that fast, it would take him one hundred sixty thousand years to get to there. Knowing that he couldn't overcome the limitation of traveling faster than light, after an hour, Larry stopped journeying toward the Clouds, returned to Earth and then used a method of travel never before thought possible. In 1921 the existence of wormholes was postulated by German mathematician Hermann Weyl based, in part, on Albert Einstein's general theory of relativity, published sixteen years earlier. Wormholes are hypothetical features of space-time. If they really existed, they would serve as "shortcuts" through the vast space of the universe. In physics, space-time is a concept that combines space and time into a single continuum. It has four dimensions, with space having three—height, width, and length—and with time being the fourth, which is of a different sort from the spatial dimensions.

To better visualize a wormhole, think of space-time as a two-dimensional surface. If this surface is folded, it allows you to picture a wormhole "bridge." A real wormhole bridge, in theory, is much like a tunnel, with each of its two ends at separate points in space-time. Don't belabor it! There's no simpler, more understandable explanation. If you can't quite grasp the concept, you're not alone. If it helps, think of *Star Trek* and the *Enterprise* traveling at warp speed. Wormholes, in effect, warp space and create shortcuts from one place to another without violating the rule that nothing can go faster than the speed of light.

Armed with this knowledge, Larry disassembled his body molecule by molecule and chose a wormhole that would take him, not to the relatively nearby Magellanic Clouds, but to the Andromeda Galaxy, 2.5 million light-years away. A light-year is a measure of distance and is the number of miles light travels in a year: 5,865,696,000,000. Without the wormhole shortcut, even at light speed, it would take Larry 2.5 million years to get to Andromeda and 2.5 million to get back.

He transferred his molecules to his aura, entered the wormhole, and emerged at the other end the next day on a planet called Mandius 481. That planet had been spotted by astronomer Mandy Wright on photos taken by the Hubble telescope in 2006 and was later named after her. It lies in Andromeda's Erhowe star system in a habitable zone, is one and half times larger than Earth, and has the correct temperature range and sufficient water to support life.

Larry hesitated before reassembling himself because he wasn't sure whether Mandius 481 had an oxygen-filled atmosphere that would enable him to breathe. He searched for living things and immediately connected with countless trillions of microbes. He searched further, and although there was no advanced humanlike or even doglike life, he connected with the minds of millions of primitive creatures that were ratlike. He dubbed them wild Mandius 481 rats, or *Rattus indomitus Mandius 481*, and his aura could interact with theirs and control their thoughts, just as he could interact with and control the thoughts of the rats at home.

Larry reassembled himself and scurried toward a nearby cave. Inside were thousands of *Rattus indomitus Mandius 481*. The first thing he noticed was that, strangely, they radiated no pheromones. That upset Larry because their primitive minds made him expect he'd have incredible sex with the females. But he could detect no gender differences among them and couldn't tell which were the males and which were the females. He soon realized that all the *Rattus indomitus Mandius 481* were genetically the same, had no gender, and like hydras on Earth, reproduced asexually by growing buds on their body walls, which became miniature adults and simply broke off when they matured.

These *Rattus indomitus Mandius 481* had no fur, and their skin was pink and naked like that of the detestable humans on Earth. But they were not vicious or cruel like the humans or wild rats Larry was accustomed to, because without testosterone and estrogen incessantly driving them to mate, they were unaggressive. Their size, however, was impressive: they were all at least two feet long. They also had long, strong teeth that protruded from their mouths, even when closed, like crocodiles' teeth. With great difficulty, because of their miniscule sized brains, Larry established control over them and, as at home, selected a few to help him rule.

He selected just three, *Rattus indomitus Mandius 481 A, B,* and *C.* Their brains were much tinier than those of the rats on Earth and were constructed differently. Whereas Earth's rats' brains had enough gray matter to enlarge and make denser with his aura, the gray matter of these rats' brains was no larger than a grain of salt. They behaved not like mammals, but like colonies of insects, driven entirely by instinct. Larry could detect no independent thinking in any of them. When he penetrated the minds of A, B, and C, they all convulsed violently, and B died instantly. If only Tompkins had died so easily, Larry thought, he'd have eliminated the human who'd created the presence—and maybe the presence along with him.

Ever so gently, Larry again penetrated the minds of A and C. After a week, with much effort, he managed to enlarge their gray matter to the size of a grain of rice. It wasn't much, but it was enough to enable him to communicate with them on a very basic level. When he tried to enlarge their gray matter further, they both convulsed violently again, so he backed off.

Larry made his aura enter A and C's brains with a single, very simple thought: *Eat.* Slowly, they reacted and led him outside the cave. The landscape was spectacular with tall redwood size trees and towering plants and grasses covering every surface. This botany was not composed of wood or vegetative matter but of a rock-hard crystalline substance. The tree trunks and plant stems were blue, and all the leaves and grass blades were red or gold. The flowers were a deep multihued orange, like Mandius 481's sun, which was much nearer and hotter than Earth's. A and C fed only on the red and gold leaves and grasses because the orange flowers were toxic. They also fed on foot-long wormlike creatures that, like chameleons, constantly changed colors. The worms changed themselves to the inedible orange color whenever A and C approached in a desperate effort to fool them into thinking they were poisonous. It seldom worked. A and C devoured a half dozen of these creatures within twenty minutes.

Larry found the worms, and the red and gold leaves and grasses, to be tasty and filling. He carefully avoided eating anything that A and C avoided. Although the vegetation was crystalline, the saliva in his mouth quickly melted it, and the worms, though horrible-looking, were firm and meaty. They were certainly no worse than the rotting meat and fish and other putrid leftovers from the humans' garbage cans he'd often fed upon at home.

Larry had not drunk for nearly two weeks. A desperate thirst drove him to search for water. He found that Mandius 481 had no oceans and no continents. It was one gargantuan landmass interspersed with hundreds of huge lakes connected to one another by fast-flowing rivers and streams. With A and C, he scampered to the shore of the nearest of the lakes, and they perched themselves on a flat rock with cracks and crevices filled by splashes from the lapping waves. The water was not clear and aqua-hued but an opaque milk white with oddly shaped fish rippling its surface. The largest were about three feet long and were the top aquatic predators on the planet. A and C were too big for these fish to swallow in a gulp, but Larry was the perfect size. One eyed him hungrily. It lunged, mouth agape, its huge mirrorlike teeth reflecting the bright sun directly at Larry, temporarily blinding him. That was the last thing it ever did as Larry's aura pierced its mind and the fish floated belly-up- dead instantly.

Only after A and C had drunk did Larry quench his thirst. The opaque milk-white water had a strange taste but was refreshing and cool. Less than fifty feet above the water's surface, however, the scorching hot temperature was unbearable. When Larry looked up, he noticed there were no birds or flying insects in the oddly colored purplish sky. Only the tall trees, their crystalline structure immune to Mandius 481 sun's blistering heat, rose skyward.

Larry spent days trying to increase the density of A and C's gray matter without injuring them but soon realized it would be impossible for them to help him rule over the other *Rattus indomitus Mandius 481* because their brains, even enlarged to the size of a grain of rice, were incapable of ruling anything. And, in truth, the millions of *Rattus indomitus Mandius 481* that populated the planet just weren't worth ruling. The most advanced thoughts they were capable of were *eat* and *shit*. They couldn't even think *fuck* since they were asexual.

The one saving grace of Mandius 481, aside from its spectacular scenery, was that here, two and a half million light-years from Earth, Larry never sensed any force or presence even remotely equivalent to his. A single human, even a single *Rattus norvegicus indomitus* (wild brown Earth rat) or *Rattus norvegicus diabetica* (diabetic brown Earth rat), most of which were only somewhat smarter than these rats, was more intelligent than all the *Rattus indomitus Mandius 481* combined.

Larry disassembled his body and cast himself into the wormhole to begin the one-day journey home. He pondered whether he should return to Calcutta or to the backyard shed, where his inner circle was waiting for his order to launch the first attack against humans. As he neared Earth, he wondered whether they had located Feras 3 and Feras 5. Despite their treachery, he had missed them. But mostly he thought of R-Five. The last time he'd seen him was nearly a half year ago, just before they escaped their claustrophobic little cage.

He also thought back worriedly to how the presence that was competing with him had prevented his causing Tompkins's death in AJCC's laboratory.

It never occurred to Larry that if his aura had not caused Tompkins to lose consciousness so quickly, the professor would have seen not just Larry scamper away, but also a second furry six-inch shape scampering away too—a shape with coarser, dirtier-looking hair; crookeder, yellower, and more worn teeth; and much beadier, though not unfriendly, eyes.

Larry would have seen that shape too had his senses not been so single-mindedly focused on killing Tompkins.

Chapter 21

As Larry journeyed earthward and approached the outer edge of the Milky Way, his aura detected the energy fields of warm-blooded creatures emanating from the Large Magellanic Cloud. He slowed, entered a wormhole that branched from the one he was in, and arrived there in a quarter hour.

The Large Magellanic Cloud and its sister, the Small Magellanic Cloud, are two dwarf galaxies that are so near to ours that they are actually satellites of our galaxy and revolve around it like Earth revolves around the Sun. The Large Magellanic Cloud is so close that it can be seen shimmering in the night sky from Earth's Southern Hemisphere. *Close*, when it comes to galactic distances, however, is a relative term, and traveling there from Earth at light speed would take one hundred sixty thousand years without a wormhole shortcut.

Larry arrived in the center of the Large Magellanic Cloud and hovered above a huge gaseous planet several times larger than Jupiter. It orbited a yellow dwarf star, like our sun, but had started to expand and was on its way to becoming a red giant. Red giants are dying stars that have enlarged to become enormous and are on their last legs. In a few tens of millions of years, older red giants explode, become supernovas, and then collapse in upon themselves and become black holes.

Larry focused his aura. Beneath the frozen exterior of the largest of the gaseous planet's moons, he located the energy fields of the creatures he'd detected. The moon's surface was solid ice, eight miles thick, but below the ice was a mile-deep hollow layer, then thousands of miles of rock, at whose center was a molten core. The heat from the core warmed the rock, and the rock warmed the hollow layer to a year-round temperature of seventy-five degrees. Astronomers had named this moon Luna Gigantica because it was twelve times larger than Earth's.

Larry penetrated this moon's icy shell and reassembled himself on the hollow layer's floor. He felt soil between his toes, and oxygen-rich air filled his lungs. There was no sunlight, but bioluminescent grasses, plants, and trees carpeted the ground, and thousands of bioluminescent creatures scurried about or flew through the air, illuminating the darkness. In this respect they were similar to bioluminescent deep-sea creatures on Earth, the kind that are able to use chemicals in their own bodies to light their way through the depths.

Sometimes, all at once, everything would go completely black, each plant and animal extinguishing its bioluminescence simultaneously. After a while, when the luminescence reignited, the entire hollow layer would erupt in a rainbow of colors much more spectacular than the most incredible Fourth of July fireworks imaginable. When that happened, Larry could see the weird creatures and the landscape clearly. All the animals' skins were transparent, like glass, and he could see their hearts beating and pumping blood, their lungs inhaling and exhaling, and their stomachs and intestines digesting food. Then everything would go black again, and although he could see nothing in the darkness, he was able to sense thinking minds.

Most of Luna Gigantica's animals had tiny brains with a miniscule amount of gray matter, but several colonies of enormous rodent-like animals, each at least a thousand members strong, consisted of creatures with gigantic brains that were 25 percent of their body weight. These creatures were on average about forty pounds in weight and three feet long. They were larger than even Louisiana's giant swamp rats, which are also known by the name nutria rats. They were like rat Frankensteins.

These animals couldn't see Larry in the darkness, but they could smell him. When he approached the lair of the largest of the colonies, hundreds of males took up defensive positions, shoulder to shoulder, protecting something behind them. What they were protecting was their queen, like ants and termites on Earth. She was huge—sixty pounds, three and a half feet long—and half her body consisted of uterus and birth canal, through which, every thirty minutes, she squeezed out a new *Luna rodenta gigantica*. Even the newborns were big, two pounds each, and other females immediately scooped them up so the babies could begin suckling a nutritious milklike liquid from their teats.

All the *Luna rodenta gigantica* were astonishingly intelligent, and their brains were as large and multifaceted as those of the despicable humans at home. Larry projected his aura and connected with the mind of the colony's queen, and the two of them were able to communicate on a very sophisticated level. She understood at once that he had no threatening intentions, at least for the time being, and as Larry probed more deeply, he realized that her intelligence and that of the other *Luna rodenta gigantica* was in some respects greater than human intelligence.

These rodents did not have dexterous hands or feet, and therefore they couldn't erect buildings, write things down, or make machines, but they spoke to one another in a complex language with more vocabulary words than English, they understood advanced scientific principles, and their memories could retain enormous amounts of information way beyond the capability of any human. In fact, they all retained a detailed memory of their common history, extending millions of years back to their creation story, which every one of them knew by heart. Each queen would recite that story to her colony often, adding in recent events to ensure it was up to date:

> In the beginning there was just intense heat or extreme cold. The floor of our hollow space could not be walked upon because the molten core below had not cooled sufficiently. Nor could we live high up near the ceiling, because the thick ice sheet above it radiated only intense cold. Back then, we were forced to live between these two extremes on rocky outcrops projecting from the walls, where we barely eked out an existence by eating lichens and fungi. Slowly, we learned farming, grew edible plants, and even raised herds of small animals so we'd have meat to feed upon.
>
> As the core cooled, we descended from our rocky outcrops and settled on the ground. Some of us experimented with different kinds of crops and livestock, became professional farmers, and learned how to grow the tastiest and most nutritious vegetables and fruits and to breed the meatiest

and leanest food animals. Others of us became doctors and discovered which combinations of minerals and plants could best cure illnesses and heal wounds. Others, especially queens, became scholars and memorized every detail of our history to preserve it for posterity. Many of our males, because of their size and musculature, became soldiers and protected us against any species that dared challenge us.

God created us in his image and gave us souls that survive our deaths. When one of us passes, our priests bury the body, mark the grave, and conduct funeral services. All *Luna rodenta gigantica* are God's ultimate creations and are superior to the other, lesser creations he placed in the world for us to rule over.

We have always warred against any creatures that threatened us, and we slaughtered or, even better, enslaved them.

Like the humans, Larry thought. The more he listened to this particular queen, the more he detested her. She reminded him exactly of the cruel humans on Earth.

Projecting his aura deep into her mind, he asked, "How long has your species been here? A year where I'm from is the number of days it takes my planet to revolve around our sun, three hundred sixty-five and a quarter. But down here you can't see your sun. So, how do you measure the passage of time?"

Communicating telepathically was not unfamiliar to her. The brains of these *Luna rodenta gigantica* were so advanced that they had always been able to sense the thoughts of other creatures, as this strange visitor seemingly could.

Unimpressed, she said, "I can tell you exactly how long our species has existed: five million one hundred six thousand years, four months, one week, three days, eight hours, and fifteen minutes."

"But how long are your years?" Larry inquired. "Not only can't you use a solar calendar, but also you can't use a lunar one, because you can't see the waning and waxing of your moon."

The idiot, she thought. She towered over him. *This midget is trying to impress me, although his mental powers, I am certain, cannot possibly be equivalent to mine.* This pipsqueak would be a challenge, but she'd outthink him like every other living thing she'd ever encountered. Her tone became condescending. He was just another of the lesser creatures the *Luna rodenta gigantica* were meant to rule.

"You see," she said disdainfully, "our smallest unit of time is how long the period of brightness is between when our bioluminescence goes on and when it goes off. Those periods of brightness are roughly equivalent to fifteen of your minutes. I know how long your minutes are because I can read your mind too. So, you do the math. If you can't, I'll do it for you."

As powerful as her mind was, she obviously had no idea whom she was dealing with. These *Luna rodenta gigantica* had arrogantly convinced themselves they were the most impressive things in the universe, when in fact they were almost as inferior to Larry as everything else. His face contorted in disgust at her haughtiness, and he increased the power of his aura, taking total control of her thoughts. He did that to all the *Luna rodenta gigantica* queens. They ferociously resisted, so he projected his aura more forcefully, intentionally inflicting pain. They could do nothing to relieve their torment, and he made them lie writhing for hours, begging for mercy.

He enjoyed their suffering. *If they truly believe God exists,* he thought, *let them understand that he is Larry.*

Chapter 22

Larry left Luna Gigantica and penetrated the boundary of the Milky Way. He passed near the constellation Libra, twenty and a half light-years from Earth, where he hovered over a planet called Gliese 581g. In 2008, that planet had been detected by astronomers after a decade of scanning using radial velocity measurements and a high-resolution spectrometer. Further observations convinced them that Gliese 581g had gravity strong enough to hold an oxygen-rich atmosphere, had plenty of water, and had a temperature mild enough to support life.

Larry cast his aura and immediately sensed the presence of tens of thousands of humanoid-type beings populating the surface of Gliese 581g. He was still consumed with rage by the arrogance of the *Luna rodenta gigantica* queens and decided to find out whether these beings, like them and the despicable humans at home, also deserved his contempt. God help them if they did. He'd be merciless and cause them intense pain too.

The humanoids lived in tribes, each about three hundred strong, and their' bodies, although not their faces, were covered with thick black hair. Larry reassembled his molecules in the camp of one of the tribes and scurried among them. The males and females looked exactly alike with an average height of nine feet. Their shoulders and their girth were twice as broad as a person's. Their feet were the size of snowshoes, so Larry had to move nimbly to avoid being trampled. Their brains were quite large but were as primitive as a Neanderthal's. They seemed to take no notice of him or of the multitude of other small creatures wandering alongside him and jostling him. There were hundreds of these small creatures everywhere he looked.

The small mammalian creatures, about the same size as Larry, with pink eyes and white fur, and walking on all fours, were unmistakably ratlike. They seemed domesticated and, at least outwardly, showed no fear of the giant humanoids who trod above them. Larry observed that whenever one of the *Gliese humanoid 581g* walked by, these ratlike creatures simply hurriedly moved out of the way, clucking to themselves in annoyance like farm-bred chickens on Earth.

Using his aura, Larry learned that the tribes kept very much to themselves, isolated from one another by towering mountain ranges, broad rivers and lakes, and vast forests. Only a rare few, he realized, would ever in their lifetimes meet up with members of a different tribe.

Everywhere, the landscape was carpeted with plants and trees that were an earthlike green—chlorophyll based—and spewing out a great deal of oxygen. The oxygen-rich air supported dozens of animal species, many of which were even larger than the humanoids. These species were very similar to the Earth's herbivorous mammals that had died off and become extinct during the last ice age: mammoths, mastodons, giant bison, deer, beaver, camel. and oxen. There were also several carnivorous species, including monstrosities that looked like giant sloths, twenty feet tall; cats that looked like saber-toothed tigers, twice the size of modern-day lions; and vicious horrors that looked like gargantuan bears, nearly as tall as the sloths.

Larry observed that although these creatures grazed and prowled very near the humanoids' camp, sometimes even within the camp, the carnivores showed not the slightest interest in feeding upon them or attacking them, even though the humanoids were unarmed and not a one carried a club, spear, or bow. Equally surprising, the carnivores showed no interest in preying upon any of the large herbivorous creatures either, yet they seemed healthy and incredibly well-fed.

In fact, the carnivores and humanoids were so unhungry that when Larry tried to read their minds to learn what they ate, he could detect no thought of feeding in any of them. It was as though they all knew, without a doubt, that their appetites would be instantly satiated when necessary.

It was morning, midsummer, and about forty-five degrees, considerably cooler than the temperature Larry was accustomed to during the same season on Earth. This accounted for why all the creatures on Gliese 581g had thick fur, including the ratlike ones. He found he could connect with these ratlike mammals' tiny brains, but they were very simple and, therefore, difficult to read. They didn't even communicate much with each other because they had no language, not even primitive squeaks and snarls. The only sounds they made were chicken-like clucks, slightly different for each one, which they used to identify themselves to each other. All they did was continuously nibble away at nuggets of some foul-smelling feed that had been prepared for them and placed in troughs.

Larry next probed the minds of the *Gliese humanoid 581g* and found a glimmer of intelligence in them. The one with the largest brain that had the most gray matter was their leader, and he was also taller and broader than most of them. Using sounds that were more like low roars and growls than like speech, he signaled the others to start the morning's first activity. All at once, the entire tribe walked to a lake near the edge of the camp, the females carrying their young in pouches like marsupials, and began bathing. For a half hour they cleaned themselves thoroughly, using handfuls of sand to scrub their bodies with. Larry hadn't noticed the pouches before because they were hidden under the thick hair on the humanoid females' bellies.

The next activity, at what would be nine thirty in the morning on Earth, was sex, which the leader initiated by mounting a random female. These humanoids did not have permanent mates, and all the adults repeatedly had intercourse with multiple partners. It was like an orgy that they participated in more for pleasure than to reproduce. When extended, the males' penises were enormous, but Larry hadn't noticed them either because, like the females' pouches, they were hidden under thick hair. After the orgy, the males rested while the females gathered up their young, which they'd removed from their pouches so they could comfortably engage in the sex, and resumed caring for them.

An hour later the leader roused himself and loudly growled something. All the humanoids except the females with young followed him outside the camp, where they began collecting armloads of fallen logs, fallen branches, and dead brush. None of the large carnivores eyed them threateningly though they could have easily killed the humanoids if they wanted to. Larry was shocked when several of the saber-toothed-tiger-like cats snuggled up against some of the humanoids and purred, hoping to be petted. Some of the giant bearlike creatures did the same, affectionately licking the humanoids' faces, yipping like puppy dogs.

The sky was a deep blue, and the temperature had warmed to fifty degrees. Gargantuan predatory-looking birds with fifteen-foot wingspans circled above, but they showed no interest in eating either. They just soared and never dove, occasionally alighting in treetops to preen. The humanoids reentered their camp, put the wood they'd collected into stone-lined pits, and carefully, in the centers of the pits, assembled tinder nests of bark and dry brush. The males then positioned the tips of pointed branches on flat stones and spun the branches rapidly until the friction created sparks and the sparks ignited the tinder nests. The females tended the fires as the wood burned and slowly transformed into glowing beds of coals.

The males, next, refilled the feed troughs of the *Gliese rattus 581g* with fresh nuggets, which the rats gathered around and began nibbling. Larry, who was starving, joined in. Although the nuggets stank somewhat, he found them delicious. It didn't bother him that occasionally a white hair became stuck in his teeth.

Gliese 581g's sun neared its highest point in midafternoon and the temperature rose to fifty-five degrees. The humanoids sunbathed in the growing warmth, but when the sun reached its apex, unexpectedly, Larry sensed the mood of the tribe changing. He sensed the mood of the giant-sloth-like monstrosities, the saber-toothed-tigerlike cats, the giant bearlike horrors, and the gargantuan predatory-looking birds changing too. He also sensed the mood of the white-furred *Gliese rattus 581g* changing. And suddenly, fear—fear beyond imagining—seized all the rats, including Larry.

Larry felt a slimy liquid running down his neck and back. He looked up. Two of the humanoids were standing over him, drooling. One drew its lips back, exposing double rows of five-inch-long fangs on both the upper and lower jaws. The other's foot-long tongue, rough as steel wool, lolled out, licking its lips. They both sniffed the air. They perked up their ears. They gazed excitedly at the ground—at the rats! Retractable, scimitar-sharp claws sprang from their fingers. Their eyes turned bloodred. Their mouths curled into sneers, and they howled in an eardrum-piercing way like werewolves.

They attacked. Larry, despite all his powers, trembled in terror and fled for his life. He hid in a crevice on the side of a boulder and watched the scene as it unfolded. It was a hundred times worse than his worst nightmare.

With their claws, the humanoids pierced the *Gliese rattus 581g* through their rectums, two with each hand, and carried them, writhing in agony, to the firepits. They preferred cooked meat, but some were unable to wait and ripped the rats' heads off with their teeth. Blood spurted from the humanoids' fanged mouths as Larry heard the rats' skulls crunching. Thousands were carried to the firepits still alive, and the males speared them with spits that could hold fifteen each like shish kebab. The spits were held three feet above the charcoal beds and rotated by the females as the rats roasted, screaming in pain. It took a full minute for the heat to kill them. The humanoids yelped with pleasure as they died.

There was more than ample rat meat to satisfy the humanoids. And they fed the land carnivores and predatory birds the leftovers, the creatures joyfully purring, yipping, and chirping as they ate. There was even enough to satisfy the twenty-foot-tall giant-sloth-like monstrosities, which could each easily devour a hundred *Gliese rattus 581g* in one sitting.

When the sadistic gluttonous display was over, the tribe's mood changed again, and they began calmly grooming each other like apes and flossing one another's teeth to remove the white hairs that had become stuck between them.

Larry had been so terrified that he'd been unable to think straight during the entire spectacle. Gradually, the nightmare he had just beheld ignited anger within him, and that anger turned to pure hate. His hate transformed into a single murderous thought: *Exterminate*. He decided to exterminate, not just some of the *Gliese humanoid 581g*, but all of them. He'd exterminate the entire race. He made his aura enter the minds of every *Gliese humanoid 581g* on the planet and every land carnivore and predatory bird. He made them die much more excruciatingly than the slowly roasting *Gliese rattus 581g* had. Compared to the torture he inflicted, Tomás de Torquemada and Adolf Hitler were amateurs. He made their capillaries and veins burst one by one. He made their kidneys and livers burst. He made their eyes slowly swell until they exploded. He tore their tongues from their mouths and ripped their tissues from their bones. He ripped their scalps from their skulls and crushed their ovaries and balls. He made them lie writhing for hours and squealed with delight as they died. Not a one was left. Larry spared only the herbivores. Only they and the rats were left.

Larry took joy in the enormity of what he'd accomplished: total extinction of every rat-eating species on the planet. He observed their mangled bodies and thought, *The humans at home will suffer like this, but worse. Much, much worse.*

Before he reentered the wormhole, he transported a thousand of the *Gliese rattus 581g* from every corner of the planet to the humanoids' camp and assembled them in a circle. Painstakingly, he enlarged the gray matter of their brains a bit and taught them how to survive by eating worms and insects instead of the foul-smelling nuggets the humanoids had been making from the corpses of the *Gliese rattus 581g*. Never again would they be forced to be cannibals, and never again would they be so abused. No rat anywhere would. Never again!

It was time for rats to feed on human corpses.

PART VI

VENGEANCE

Chapter 23

Larry transported himself through a space-time wormhole to the backyard shed, where his inner circle was waiting. Having succeeded in traveling to other galaxies, his arrogance was at its height, and he seriously considered insisting that henceforth they address him as "Lord" or "Master." To bring himself back down to earth (no pun intended), he ratcheted the reptilian part of his mind down a notch because if he couldn't restrain his lizard-like tongue from slithering out and ranting about visiting other galaxies, then every one of them would think he was psycho.

During his travels, Larry's contempt for all creatures humanlike had enormously deepened, as had the disdain he felt for most of his inner circle since, except for Feras 1 and Feras 7, they still feared his plan to launch a war against people. They were cowards and morons.

Feras indomitus 1 said, "Sir, we thought something happened to you. We searched everywhere, but it was like you dropped off the planet."

Larry chuckled inside but managed not to start talking about the *Rattus indomitus Mandius 481*, the *Luna rodenta gigantica 12*, and the detestable *Gliese humanoid 581g* he'd seen. Although he found it difficult to control himself, he felt it best not to reveal that he'd traveled millions of light-years away, because then his generals, several of whom already seriously questioned his sanity, would be even more terrified of him which, for now, he wanted to prevent.

"Morons ..., uh, I mean, Generals, have you located Three and Five?"

"Yes," Two responded. "We have them in custody."

He breathed deeply, relieved. "How did they avoid us for so long? Were they being helped?"

"Not likely," replied Seven, the little shit. "They were hiding among your and Three's litters that survived the humans' difethialone and indandione poisons."

"How can you be sure they didn't have help?"

"Because I took it upon myself to have them waterboarded, sir, and believe me, they would have talked by now."

Larry watched Seven intently. Despite how much he disliked the little prick, this was the part of him he enjoyed.

"Waterboarded? You actually waterboarded them?"

"Yes, sir. Repeatedly, for three days nonstop, over and over. Separately, together, in the same room, in different rooms! They would have broken and sung like canaries if they had anything to tell."

Larry turned to One. "Well then, are we battle-ready?"

"Sir, we were battle-ready six weeks ago when you left, but, um"—he was almost afraid to say it—"a problem has arisen."

From his tone, Larry knew immediately that there was more than just a problem. Something, he sensed, basic to his attack plan had gone seriously wrong.

"What problem?"

"Sir, I don't know where you've been or whether you've been monitoring what's been going on around here, but—"

One was right. *God,* Larry thought, *I've been millions upon millions of light-years away for more than a month. Earth could have exploded and disappeared and I wouldn't have known it.*

"… the humans have been tipped off. They're onto us," One continued. "They know we're planning to attack en masse and have armed themselves with poison guns. They've been issued protective suits and oxygen masks to shield themselves from the difethialone and indandione when they spray it at us."

The idiots, Larry thought. *The humans are so simple-minded that they actually believe that is going to save them.*

"And, sir," Feras 2 interjected, "they've developed even more deadly poisons. While you've been gone they've sprayed tons of third-generation poisons into our dens too. We've suffered three hundred fifty thousand casualties already."

Using his aura, Larry immediately analyzed the chemical composition of those poisons and began altering the physiology of the more than one million rats that had not been killed to give them immunity.

Two added, trembling, "And the casualties included hundreds more of your children. At most, twenty-five are left."

Hearing that, Larry's blood boiled, his eyes bulged, and a single murderous thought entered his mind, the same single thought that had entered his mind on Gliese 581g: *Exterminate!* He remembered how easily he'd killed the entire race of humanoid 581g along with every other predatory species on the planet. He remembered the delight he felt as they lay dying, writhing in pain. Larry had to summon every ounce of his willpower to prevent himself from acting on that thought.

Yet again, there was something stopping him from acting on it, even if he wanted to, something that frightened him much more than the idea of attacking the humans frightened most of his generals. The powerful presence, he realized, had penetrated his mind and was inside him now, wrestling with his aura, preventing it from being unleashed like the angel in Genesis that wrestled all night with Jacob.

In Genesis the Bible says that Jacob, after living twenty years in the town of Haran and wedding Leah, and then Leah's sister, Rachel, and siring ten children by them and two by their maids, decided to return to the Promised Land. On the way one evening, he found himself alone, his entourage having obeyed his order to march on ahead. An imposing stranger approached, and to back him off, Jacob began grappling with him. The stranger was not human but a supernatural being possessing remarkable strength. After a wrestling match that lasted all night, Jacob was grievously injured. He walked with a limp for the rest of his life.

That's the magnitude of strength Larry felt emanating from the presence. Larry knew, despite his aura's awesome ability to transport him to other galaxies, read minds, force other living things to do his bidding, and even alter the physiology of other creatures, he was no match for it. If he persisted in acting out his thought to exterminate, it would cripple him or even kill him.

"Are you all right?" *Feras rattus indomitus 1* asked. Until now, One had never seen fright or the slightest discomfort etched on Larry's face. Even Seven was shocked as Larry grimaced, clearly in pain. But One, Seven, and the others noticed something else. A strange glimmer shone in Larry's eyes, and a sneer curled his lips. The presence, while wrestling with Larry deep in his mind, had been forced to reveal itself, not entirely, but enough so that Larry began to understand what it was.

While deep in his head, the presence didn't just fight with Larry, but also spoke telepathically to him, like the queen on Luna Gigantica 12. The cadence of its speech was familiar. What's more, Larry was temporarily able to get a fix on the place where the presence was located. He cast his aura toward that place, and it was the filthy little cage at the University of Vermont in which he'd been imprisoned for so long.

In fact, Aubrey and Becky were standing in front of that cage now, checking to see if his former cage-mates *Rattus norvegicus diabetica 1, 2, 3,* and *4* had eaten all the food they'd been given with the experimental baldness medication mixed in. Without Larry around constantly bathing them in his aura, the gray matter of their minds had reverted to the pathetically small size it had been before the energy healers arrived. The rats could no longer speak. They could barely even think. They were nothing more than stupid little lab rats again.

But another of Larry's former cage-mates was there too, with coarser, dirtier-looking hair; crookeder, yellower, and more worn teeth; and much beadier, though not unfriendly, eyes. This cage-mate could speak fluently, albeit in a slow and halting manner, and within its body, the ability of the symbiotic living being growing there to self-adjust, almost as if it could think by itself, was enormous.

Chapter 24

There they were, his former cage-mates—*Rattus norvegicus diabetica 1, 2, 3,* and *4* and R-Five—meekly submitting to their daily routines as lab rats. Except for R-Five, their brains had reverted to their ridiculously small, but normal, rat size, and they weren't even aware that a year prior Larry had escaped or had ever been trapped in cage 28 with them.

The experimental baldness medication was working. In addition to causing blood vessels to hemorrhage, the stress that lab animals suffer from being confined often causes hair loss. Patches of once bald skin on all Larry's former cage-mates' bellies, loins, and cheeks were now covered with fresh fur. To gauge the effectiveness of the baldness medication, several ALATs, with Aubrey and Becky supervising, were taking photos of the rats and comparing them with ones taken previously. The next step would be human testing. Then, if the medication worked on people, it would put Rogaine and all other brands of baldness treatment out of business.

Larry tried mightily to retain the fix he'd gotten on the location from where the presence was emanating, but it not only had prevented him from acting out his thought to exterminate, but also stopped him from remembering where it, the presence, was coming from. Larry struggled with all his strength to remember, but the temporary fix he'd gotten on the location slowly ebbed from his mind. His aura, though, remained as terrifyingly powerful as ever, and he could easily overhear Aubrey and Becky's conversations and also read their thoughts if he so desired.

Becky said, "Aubrey, the mayor wants to meet with us about the city's rat problem. The rats have begun rampaging through the streets and injuring people. The Rodent Control Department has already killed hundreds of thousands, but the mayor is still not satisfied."

"I know," Aubrey replied. "According to the newspapers, large groups of rats began streaming out of their sewers weeks ago, frightening everyone. It's very strange. They come out, run amok for a while, and then disappear into their dens and sewers again."

"I've never heard of rats behaving that way before, Aubrey. What do you make of it?"

"I don't know. It's like something's driving them. Maybe they've been infected with some crazy rodent disease, because the news reports say they've been frothing at the mouth like rabid dogs. Maybe that's it?"

*

The rodent control manager, Tom Garret, was sitting with his field chiefs. The chief in charge of managing the rat population in Willow Park said, "Tom, yesterday morning something I can't explain started happening. The rats aren't being affected by the last batch of difethialone and indandione we sprayed at them. And they're not being affected much by the new third-generation poisons either."

"My exterminators are telling me the same thing," the chief responsible for rat control on the city's north side said. "The poisons simply aren't killing them anymore. The last batch we bought must be defective."

"I don't think so," said the chief in charge of the south side. "One of my exterminators removed his mask for a second to adjust the strap, and the poison fumes almost killed him. He convulsed violently and started bleeding from his nose and mouth. He's in intensive care right now."

They compared notes for a long time. Tom Garret called the company from which he'd purchased the poisons, and they assured him that the ingredients in the new batch were the same as the ingredients in the batches that had killed three hundred fifty thousand of the city's rats over the past two months.

"Tom," the field chief in charge of rat control along the canal said, "we have to accept that there's nothing wrong with the poisons. It's something else."

"Are you crazy? I don't care what the company that sold us the stuff says. Of course there's something wrong with it. There's got to be."

"Tom, I'm telling you, it's not the poisons," the canal field chief repeated.

*

One of the ALATs walked over with a cell phone to where Aubrey and Becky were talking. "Becky, you'd better take this. It's from Rodent Control Manager Garret. He says it's an emergency."

Becky spoke to him for ten minutes. When she was finished, she said, "Aubrey, Tom Garret wants to see us. He's beside himself."

"Did he say why? What's wrong?"

"Yes. He's in a panic. He says the poisons aren't working anymore. He says that somehow, the rats have all become immune."

*

Aubrey and Becky walked into Tom Garret's office. Bob Morris, now the Three R's Committee veterinarian at UVM, having recently moved up from his position as a vet tech to a fully credentialed DVM, and whom both knew well, was sitting next to Tom with a stern expression on his face.

"Sit down," Bob said without introductions or hellos. "We've got some questions.

"Here's the situation. As Tom told you, Becky, the poisons aren't affecting the rats anymore, but we know the poisons aren't defective because they're still deadly to people. I just finished doing some quick blood tests on two rats we trapped this morning, and incredibly their body chemistry has changed. I'm assuming that's why they've become immune."

"Are you sure? That just can't be," Becky responded.

"Yes, and I discovered something else. After I saw the results of the blood tests, I pulled out some records concerning the genus of rats you're using at the university's laboratory for the baldness medicine research. They're all *Rattus norvegicus diabetica*, that is, brown diabetic rats. Did you

105

know that? They were bred that way, and several thousand were delivered to your laboratory about a year ago. They all have type 1 diabetes."

Becky shifted uncomfortably in her seat. "I … I didn't know. But how couldn't I? I've been working with those rats ever since they arrived."

"You're not the only one. I asked around. The professor conducting the testing of the new baldness medication, the chairman of the university's biology department, and nobody on the Three R's Committee, including me, knew that either."

Becky thought back. For a moment, vague memories of injecting the rats with something stirred in her mind.

Aubrey, in the meantime, although listening intently, sat stone silent.

"And there's more. The records say that a Professor Robert Tompkins— no one remembers him either—was doing experiments on these *Rattus norvegicus diabetica* with a new kind of insulin and that early on they became sick with hemorrhaging blood vessels. To cure them, another guy nobody's heard of, a Doctor Gary Schwartz, brought in energy healers led by a Native American man named Moxus. Does any of this sound familiar? Becky? Aubrey?"

They both stared at him.

"Well, let me tell you something, it should sound familiar because you, Becky, were the manager of Tompkins's insulin experiment, and you, Aubrey, were the next in command."

Becky simply could not believe what she was hearing. She tried to answer and began moving her mouth, but no words came out. Aubrey didn't do even that. She remained stone silent.

Bob continued, "And get this: this Professor Tompkins, I tracked him down. He's doing diabetes research at some laboratory in Calcutta with the help of your boss, Simona Gupta, who's there with him now, and an ALAT named Ron Carter. I dug through your records, and according to them, Becky, this Carter used to work for you. Ever hear of him?"

Becky's mouth began to twitch, blood rushed to her face, and beads of perspiration formed on her brow. She tried to stand but grew faint and almost collapsed to the floor. One of the field chiefs brought her some water.

"Now goddammit, you two, don't look at me like teenage girls about to cry. I want some fucking answers, and I want them now! What the hell is going on around here?"

Chapter 25

Becky and Aubrey were not just colleagues, they were also close friends. As they rode by taxi back to the UVM lab, Becky was so numb that she was still barely able to speak. She was in clinical shock. While she leaned heavily against the back seat's headrest, Aubrey dabbed at her forehead with a damp cloth.

Becky recovered enough strength to start perusing the thick copy of the lab's records that Bob Morris had given her, which included, she dazedly realized, more than a hundred pages in her own handwriting. She looked at her first entry, dated just shy of twelve months ago: "2,860 rats, species *Rattus norvegicus diabetica*, received today at 11:15 a.m. Bred by C. River Labs. Transported and unloaded at west receiving dock by D. Services. Inventory completed by R. Carter 1:45 p.m. Health status check supervised by A. Adams. Nine rejected: five with broken teeth, four with glazed eyes."

"*Rattus norvegicus diabetica*, bred by C. River Labs"! "*Rattus norvegicus diabetica*, bred by C. River Labs"! Reading that, written in her own script, jogged something. Becky squeezed her eyes shut, trying to remember, forcing herself to. She recalled that Charles River Laboratories International Inc., a multibillion-dollar biotech company, was the largest breeder in the United States and that Direct Services Inc., using a fleet of specially designed trucks, was the largest transporter of lab animals in the United States. Remembering only that, however, was no big deal. Charles River routinely sold lab animals to the university, and Direct Services routinely delivered them. Just yesterday Becky had seen a truck with the Direct Services logo unloading crates of mice all tagged "Charles River."

She studied her next entry, dated two days later: "As per Prof. Tompkins, 1 mg of insulin formula PRT to be administered four times daily to test group *R. diabetica* in cages 1–150; 1 mg insulin formula Humalog (R) to be administered to control group *R. diabetica* in cages 151–300, same frequency."

Humalog(R), she knew, meant Humalog Regular. It was the most frequently prescribed insulin around the world. And PRT insulin, she recalled, was experimental.

Becky, remembering another thing, searched for her entry dated two months after the PRT testing had begun, June 12: "LATs report hemorrhaging capillaries in more than 90 percent of test and control group rats. Professor Tompkins to meet with the Three R's Committee and recommend a solution. For now, switch all rats to extreme low-carb diets and discontinue insulin injections for seventy-two hours."

This was insane! How could she have forgotten all this? She was meticulously well trained, highly intelligent, and exceptionally competent. That this information had simply slipped her mind was impossible.

The next entry was one in Aubrey's handwriting. Becky positioned the page in front of her, pointing to it. Aubrey read: "June 15. Dr. Gary Schwartz with sixteen assistants, whom he calls 'energy healers,' arrived in the morning. Genuine energy healers began hand-waving treatment on rats in the test group in cages 21–28; sham energy healers, on the control group, cages 29–36."

Dr. Gary Schwartz. The name seemed familiar. Energy healers. Becky remembered that too. And test cage group cages 21–28? *Cage 28,* her mind shouted, *was Larry's!*

And suddenly, everything she'd forgotten came rushing back. All that had happened had been locked in her memory, but some strange force, like a straitjacket, had restrained her from retrieving it. For Aubrey, however, nothing came rushing back, because she'd never forgotten the PRT testing. In fact, she hadn't forgotten anything. That's why she'd sat stone silent in Tom Garret's office while Becky, in contrast, had come close to passing out.

The strange force simply hadn't affected Aubrey. But why? How couldn't it have?

*

The moment the taxi dropped off Becky and Aubrey, they walked to cage 28, where *Rattus norvegicus diabetica 1–5* (with *Rattus norvegicus diabetica 5* being R-Five) were. It was interesting that they both thought of R-Five as different from the others without ever having discussed it before. They also realized at once that Larry, whose number was six, wasn't there, which caused them to remember the times they stood watching his cage thinking he and One, Two, Three, Four, and Five were talking. They recalled how Larry seemed so much more intelligent than the others and the humanlike expressions that often crossed his face.

Larry was watching Aubrey and Becky intently. Although he wasn't in the cage, he was nearby, in the backyard shed with his new inner circle, *Rattus feras indomitus 1, 2, 6, 7,* and *8*. Aubrey and Becky sensed him and searched the cages adjoining cage 28 thinking that maybe he'd been moved. What they sensed, however, was his aura radiating from the shed two miles away. He was implanting suggestions in their minds that they go to Bob Morris and persuade him that the reason the city's rats had started rampaging and become immune was that they had come down with a strange disease. That was untrue, the truth being that Larry had altered their physiology to make them immune and the rats' rampages were actually rehearsals for his planned mass attacks on humans.

Although Larry had lost his fix on the presence, the presence had not lost its fix on him. Larry suddenly felt it inside him again, fighting his aura, this time preventing the false suggestions he was attempting to implant into Becky and Aubrey from taking hold.

The presence, however, wanted them to know the truth, that the attack of Larry's rat army was imminent. It wanted them to know that they and every person in the city were in peril.

In fact, if they didn't figure out how to defend themselves, they'd all be writhing in excruciating pain or be dead, and the few who were not would wish they were by the next morning.

Chapter 26

Larry would give the order to launch the first mass assault in less than twenty-four hours, and the humans, seeing that their difethialone, indandione, and more advanced third-generation poisons were no longer working, still had no plan to fend his rat army off.

The situation was so dire that an array of high-ranking government officials and UVM staff assembled in Mayor Perkins's office. The director of the Centers for Disease Control, the Vermont governor's chief of staff, the Vermont commissioner of health, and the Republican and Democratic leaders of the Burlington City Council attended. Rodent Control Manager Tom Garret and his field chiefs; Bob Morris and the other members of the Three R's Committee; Becky Byers; and Aubrey Adams were also present. Simona Gupta, dean of UVM's Biomedical Research Department, had been invited, of course, but could not attend because she was still in Calcutta. Assistant Dean Edgar Palo attended in her place.

The mayor convened the meeting:

"Gentlemen, ladies, as I understand it, large hordes of rats numbering in the several thousands began streaming from the sewers two months ago. I can confirm this because I've seen them with my own eyes. Three hundred fifty people have suffered rat bites since then, and more than half of these occurred during the past week. The rats have become frighteningly aggressive and, what's more, immune to the most advanced poisons available. I've asked you here today to help devise a strategy to deal with this catastrophe before it gets worse. You've all been introduced and briefed. And now we'll hear from Rodent Control Manager Tom Garret, whose department's been closest to the problem. Tom, tell us what's been going on?"

"All right, Mr. Mayor. The latest information is that this morning alone, thirty more people have been bitten. The rats have completely lost their fear of people, and when anyone approaches, they savagely attack. There is no precedent for this kind of behavior. Even during the black death, which in the fourteenth century killed some seventy-five million people, existing records confirm that disease-carrying rats seldom inflicted bites. In fact, the plague was not transmitted by rat bites but by the bites of fleas infected with a bacterium called *Yersinia pestis* living on their fur. It all started in China when rats that were infested with these fleas were brought to Europe via merchant ships."

"What has that got to do with our problem, Tom?"

"I bring it up, Mr. Mayor, because the only good news I have to report is that none of the nearly four hundred people who were bitten have become ill. I mean, some of their bites became infected, but that's it. There's no evidence of communicable disease of any type and certainly no plague."

"Well, that's just great," chimed in the Republican leader of the city council, "but a hundred people in my district have been bitten, four so badly that they were hospitalized. And what's this insanity I'm hearing that the rats have become immune to the difethialone and other poisons all about? We paid seventy-five thousand dollars for that stuff."

"I know it sounds insane," Morris said, interjecting "and I couldn't believe the results of my own tests, but I'm telling you, the rats' physiology and chemistry has changed."

The CDC director added, "I had my people rerun the blood tests you performed, Mr. Morris. At first, I thought you were nuts, but your results checked out. No CDC scientist in the country has ever seen anything like it. They tell me no living organism can mutate that fast—not insects, bacteria, or even viruses."

The state's commissioner of health remarked, "I've seen those results too, but how the hell could their chemistry have changed just like that, like magic? I'm a scientist—in fact, I'm a prizewinning biologist for my research on genetic mutations—and I believe there's got to be a rational explanation."

The mayor said, "Like it or not, that's what's happened, so let's all stop dropping our jaws in disbelief and try to come up with a plan. Tom, have the fire hoses had any effect?"

"Not much. We're using the high-pressure hoses on every fire truck in the city to spray tons of water into the sewers and the rat dens. We've drowned thousands but just don't have enough equipment to make a real dent in their numbers."

"Well," the Democratic leader said, turning to the governor's chief of staff, "can you get another twenty-five fire trucks here for us?"

Before the chief could answer, the mayor raised his hand, his palm facing the others. "Stop. That won't work. The city's water pressure can barely keep the hoses running on the fire trucks we have now."

"Gentlemen," the governor's chief of staff said, "if more trucks will help, we'll get them. But you say that the people who were bitten have not come down with any disease. Are you sure? The newspaper reports I've read say the rats are frothing from the mouth as if they're rabid. Maybe there'll be some delayed reaction from whatever's infected the damn rats?"

Bob Morris said, "Unlikely, sir. The first rat bites happened more than two months ago, and there are no reports of anyone showing the slightest symptoms. None of them have needed treatment other than for their bite wounds."

"What bothers me much more," Bob continued, "is this experimental insulin testing at the university that no one, and I mean no one, can seem to remember. You've all been briefed about it. In my opinion, that experiment has got to be tied in somehow to what's happening with the rats."

He looked over at Becky and Aubrey. "Miss Byers, Miss Adams, now would be a good time for those goddamn answers I asked you for, ladies."

They hesitated, both of them more fearful of losing their jobs now than at any time since they'd told Tompkins three quarters of a year ago that they thought Larry and his cage-mates were talking.

Becky began, saying, "Mis … Mister Mayor, Mister Morris, what I'm about to tell you is going to be much more difficult to believe than the assertion that the rats' chemistry has suddenly changed, but please hear me out." She gathered herself. "Gentlemen, the insulin-testing experiment lasted about a year. I was the laboratory animal technologist in charge of managing it, but until I read the records Mr. Morris found, I'd forgotten it ever happened. That I can't explain, but I have a theory, one I think that will clarify things. Let me—"

"A theory?" the Republican leader thundered at her. "How old are you, little lady? Twenty-four, twenty-five maybe? You don't remember you were in charge of a multimillion-dollar experiment? Do you even remember your name? your address? Mr. Morris tells me you wrote most of those records, but you somehow forgot everything? Were you and your friend over here on crack? I have daughters your age. Were you too busy shaking your butts at some party? Do you really expect us to sit here quietly and listen to your damn theory?"

The mayor shouted, "I'm running this meeting, Councilman! Unless you have something helpful to say, let her talk!"

Morris added, "Give her a chance, Councilman Peters. If you have some insight into what's been happening around here, fine, but in the meantime, what she says may be all we have to go on."

Struggling to keep her composure, Becky said, "As I was saying, the experiment lasted a year. It began when two thousand eight hundred sixty rats with type 1 diabetes were delivered to the university's laboratory. I was instructed by Professor Robert Tompkins to begin injecting a test group of those rats with a new kind of insulin he'd developed with his associate, and my boss, Professor Simona Gupta. She dubbed his insulin 'PRT.' It worked remarkably well. There were rumors that Pfizer Pharmaceuticals was negotiating with Tompkins to buy his patent for a billion dollars."

The director of the Centers for Disease Control interrupted, saying, "Has anyone asked Pfizer if they remember any of this?"

Morris said, "I checked with them last week. No one there has heard of PRT insulin or Tompkins, and no one remembers negotiating with him or anyone else at the university about anything. They were going to send a representative to this meeting, but I thought it best to keep all of this to ourselves for now."

Becky continued, "One of the problems when using laboratory animals for research, particularly mice and rats, is that the stress of being in captivity for long periods of time often causes their blood vessels to hemorrhage. That is, their capillaries begin to leak, and blood starts pooling in their body cavities. That's what happened to the diabetic rats at UVM. And their hemorrhaging was made worse by the additional stress of the constant PRT injections."

Hearing that, the entire group, even Peters, decided to pay attention. "Go on," said the CDC director.

"The hemorrhaging got so bad that many of the rats died, which threatened to ruin Tompkins's entire experiment. One day, about six months after the injections began, he hired a researcher named Gary Schwartz, who showed up with some people called 'energy healers.' You've all been briefed a little about that too. The idea was that these healers could make their own potent biochemical auras interact with the rats' tiny auras and cause the hemorrhaging to stop. They did that by waving their hands over them."

"Oh my God," Peters mumbled. "This is bullshit!"

"Anyhow," Becky said, ignoring him, "the hand-waving worked, and the rats started to recover. After the energy healers left, some of the rats, one in cage 28 in particular, whom Aubrey and I call Larry, began behaving strangely. He seemed to become amazingly intelligent, and to a lesser extent, so did his cage-mates. It got to the point where I could have sworn they were making more than just their usual squeaks and snarls but were actually talking to each other."

The commissioner of health stood up in shock. "Have you totally lost your mind? Are you crazy?" he yelled.

"Please," Morris said, "let her finish because there's more; much more. You should sit down because what Miss Byers told me before you got here, sir, is going to make you faint. I can barely say it myself without thinking I've gone crazy, but according to her, this Larry's aura became so powerful that he developed the ability to telepathically read minds."

The entire group stood up, even the mayor, who said, "I thought you were a serious researcher, Bob."

"Believe me, Mr. Mayor, I am. And if you'll force yourself to listen just a little longer, you'll—"

Becky wanted to make sure that what she was about to say would sound sensible, but she couldn't wait. Her words came spilling out: "Larry grew so intelligent and his aura so powerful that he developed the ability not only to read minds but also to influence the thoughts and actions of all living creatures. I have no idea what he may be capable of now, but I do know that as his powers increased, he began to deeply detest people for keeping him captive and constantly injecting him with needles. And I think it was Larry who ended Tompkins's experiment. He felt threatened by the PRT insulin."

No one talked or moved, or even breathed, for a full minute. There was a shocked silence. Councilman Peters finally erupted in anger. "Are you hallucinating, Miss Byers? Do you think you're sitting around at some goddamn crack party with your fucking friends?"

Edgar Pilo, assistant dean of UVM's Biomedical Research Department, who hadn't spoken a word until this moment, said, "Miss Byers, you're terminated, effective immediately." He grabbed his cell phone and dialed. "I'm calling the campus police right now. I'm going to ask that you be taken into custody and not released until we're sure you haven't altered or stolen any records."

"But she has proof!" Morris shouted. "Show them!"

Becky reached into her pocketbook and pulled out a plastic case containing a DVD. She said, "The university's animal laboratory has security cameras all over the place. This is a portion of what was recorded by one of these cameras, showing cage 28 and the cages around it. It's dated Friday, August 30, 2023, with a time of seven o'clock in the evening." She handed the DVD to the mayor, who inserted it into the ROM slot of the computer on his desk. He positioned the screen so everyone could see.

When the DVD began to play, it showed Larry with incredibly thick and lustrous fur and long, sharp, perfectly shaped teeth. It showed Becky in a trance walking toward his cage. It showed her trying to stop herself from unhinging the latch, but unhinging it nevertheless. And it showed Larry walking through the door, haughtily erect on only his two hind legs and not on all fours.

Sweat poured from the CDC director's face.

Edgar Pilo's phone slipped from his grasp.

"Keep watching," Morris said.

The DVD went on to show the other rats also escaping the cage. It showed Larry moving his mouth as if talking and the others moving their mouths as if they were talking too. Next, they saw Larry climb atop a cabinet and study a map on the wall. They saw him look for a long time at the part of map showing the cages where the females were kept. And they saw through it all the humanlike expressions crossing his face.

They watched the entire DVD. When it was finished, not a soul in the room thought Becky Byers was insane anymore.

The commissioner of health, clearing his throat several times, asked, "Why do you think this Larry rat felt threatened by the PRT insulin?"

Becky had pushed her credibility to the breaking point and was afraid to say another word. But she blurted, "Be … because the PRT became con … conscious. It became ali—"

"Alive," Aubrey said, finishing the sentence for her. "It morphed into a conscious, sentient being—a presence—within the bodies of the diabetic rats that had been injected with it. This presence exists now and is as powerful as Larry's aura."

They all looked at her.

"The presence is fighting the aura and trying to stop it from killing people. Gentlemen, it's not a disease that's causing the rats to attack; it's Larry!"

But there was something else, something as yet inexplicable and undetected. Becky knew there was some third force in play, umpiring the struggle between the aura and the presence, ensuring that neither would become dominant. She wasn't sure how or why she knew, but she knew.

For a split second, her eyes locked deeply with Aubrey's and Bob Morris's, and in that moment she realized that they knew too.

Chapter 27

Not long after Gary Schwartz had brought in the energy healers who cured the hemorrhaging capillaries of the *Rattus norvegicus diabetica*, he became director of the Laboratory for Advances in Consciousness and Health at the University of Arizona in Tucson, as well as director of energy healing for Tucson's Canyon Ranch Resorts. The spectacular success of Moxus and the other healers had convinced him that energy medicine, heretofore practiced primarily in the Far East and by Native Americans, could be developed to the point where it might cure diseases that Western medicine had failed to.

Tucson was the perfect location for Gary's research because the Hopi, Navajo, and Apache, and other, lesser-known Arizona tribes, had been practicing energy medicine for centuries. He was able to draw upon the knowledge of these Native Americans, many of whom lived within walking distance of the university, and test their methods in the modern laboratories there.

Gary Schwartz had an outlandish idea. He theorized that occasionally persons were born possessing auras so extraordinary that even Moxus's paled in comparison. Moses, Confucius, Buddha, Jesus, the Prophet Muhammad, and Joan of Arc, perhaps, were such persons. Their auras were so potent that millions of people were enveloped by them and believed these persons were godlike.

When these individuals died, their bodies perished, but according to Dr. Schwartz, the powerful auras they'd emanated continued living on as dispersed energy fields. Over the millennia, their auras dispersed further and diminished in strength, but the remnants of their auras, particularly of the more recent of these godlike persons such as Jesus, still powerfully influence billions of their followers. The same is obviously true of the Prophet Muhammad and probably Joan of Arc. How else can we explain how a seventeen-year-old peasant girl, born January 6, 1412, without education, wealth, physical strength, or political power, and seemingly by way of sheer charisma alone, was able to persuade thousands of battle-hardened men to follow her, become leader of the French army, and eventually defeat the English, ending the Hundred Years' War?

Dr. Schwartz's theories, however, have often been criticized and sometimes ridiculed by other researchers. Most of his colleagues, nonetheless, gave him credit for deeply exploring the characteristics of auras and trying to quantify their strength. Although many found his conclusions fantastical, the results of some of his experiments have been confirmed, as follows:

- First, sometimes when energy healers wave their hands over small, stressed lab animals, it really does reduce the hemorrhaging of their capillaries.

- Second, close family members, particularly mothers and their children, can often detect the energy fields emanating from each other's minds and beating hearts, sometimes through closed doors and across large distances.

- Third, there's no doubt that the energy fields emanating from the minds of people in large crowds often powerfully interact, sometimes dangerously and violently. It's called "mob mentality."

- Fourth, acupuncture, practiced by Chinese doctors since antiquity and now throughout the world, redirects the flow of energy through invisible channels within the body and often successfully reduces pain, heals injuries, and cures diseases.

In the grand scheme of things, however, the above-described energy fields are relatively small and weak, but the research of physicists and astronomers has dramatically confirmed the existence and almost unfathomable strength of a particular energy field, not just millennia after, but millions of millennia after its source died off.

Think back to what you learned in high school about nuclear bombs: when a minute ball of uranium particles are fused together, a massive explosion occurs. The fused particles are the protons and neutrons in the nucleus of the uranium atom, and the fusion pressure causes them to split, collide with other nuclei, and set off a chain reaction.

Likewise, the big bang theory of how the universe came into existence postulates that 13.8 billion years ago, a minute ball of particles exploded with such a force that the immeasurably powerful energy field it radiated—its aura—is still expanding at breakneck speed. A portion of that energy converted into mass, which became the stars, planets, comets, quasars, and all other structures in our universe.

Einstein's formula $E = mc^2$, or rearranged $M = e/c^2$, that is, mass = energy $\cdot/\cdot$ speed of light^2, explains how that conversion occurred. It shows that mass and energy are convertible: mass can convert into energy and energy can convert into mass.

Cosmologists postulate that other big bangs have occurred and that our universe, with its billions of galaxies and trillions of stars, is just one universe among an infinite number of parallel ones. Like ours, these others all began as minute particle balls.

The force of those big bangs is incalculable, and no force even remotely equivalent has ever been generated. Larry's aura and the presence are summer breezes in comparison. But other extraordinary forces seem to exist, not nearly as powerful as the big bangs, yet degree upon degree more powerful than the aura or presence.

They are so strange that, thus far, they've been beyond human ability to detect.

Chapter 28

Simona Gupta was feverishly making notes. She'd become very much aware of the aura and the presence, and also that some inexplicable, as-yet-undetected third power was in play. Not only had Bob Morris and Becky phoned a week ago to alert her to their suspicions, but also she had been harboring her own for a long while.

She mumbled to herself as she wrote: "My patient worsening... began massive dosages of PRT too late... kidney and heart failure imminent... gangrene on lower extremities uncontrolled... amputation of right foot and all digits on left unavoidable.

"Only positive: glucose levels drastically lower, but organ damage irreversible... too extensive .... Death expected within two months."

Gupta removed her glasses, rubbed her temples, and cradled her face in her hands for a moment, her elbows resting on her slate-topped desk.

"Know now it was not R-Five who changed Tompkins's experiment testing PRT into an experiment testing baldness medication, and it was not R-Five who made everyone forget that the PRT experiments ever happened at UVM. He had no motive to. R-Five wanted PRT injections to continue so that the sentient being it created inside him, and the presence along with it, would grow strong enough to defeat Larry's aura.

"Larry, however, had a strong motive to end the PRT experiment because stopping the injections would eliminate the presence, but only if he knew Tompkins's PRT had created the presence."

And Gupta was convinced that Larry hadn't known that the PRT created the presence. In fact, it was her patient Rohan Karteray who'd told her that Larry didn't know. *But how can my patient,* she thought, *be so certain?* And if it wasn't Larry or R-Five who'd had ended the experiment, then who or what had? She answered her own question: *Something or someone much more powerful did.* And as she tried to figure out who or what, the identity of the most likely candidate came to mind.

My patient. I think it's him!

Rohan Karteray suffered from a rare form of type 1 diabetes and, to date, was the first and only human upon whom PRT had been tested. Professor Gupta, in her desperation to cure him, had instructed Rohan to inject himself with ten massive doses of it every day. Like Simona, he was of Indian descent and had been born in Gujarat, the same province she was from. He was tall yet very frail, almost as tan-skinned as Simona, and exceptionally intelligent like she was. All her life, Simona and he had enjoyed an especially close relationship. And because he had this rare form of type 1 diabetes, she was at his bedside when necessary and was always concerned about his health.

Somehow, it was Rohan who'd converted Tompkins's new insulin experiment into a mere cure-for-baldness experiment and made everyone forget that testing PRT at UVM had ever taken place.

Nevertheless, no matter how much PRT he needed and no matter what its effects, Simona would continue instructing this special patient of hers to inject himself with massive daily doses. And she'd do whatever else it took to save him.

Chapter 29

By using his aura, Larry had read the thoughts of every person at Mayor Perkins's meeting and had watched Becky's entire DVD. He knew therefore they were finally on to his plan to attack humans, but he also knew that there was little they could do to defend themselves. Only one thing he had overheard was important to him, consisting of three little words. These three words rolled deliciously off his tongue as he murmured them, which gave him incalculable joy. *Why didn't I think of those words,* Larry asked himself—*the black death*—*before?*

He was chortling, nearly choking with joy at what he knew was to come. With his aura, Larry infested the fur of every rat in his army with scores of *Yersinia pestis*–infected fleas so that in addition to suffering from hundreds of rat bites, the humans would contract the black death and suffer from that too.

Did you know that there is still no effective cure? There is a plague vaccine, but if the vaccine is given *after* you're infected, it won't work, because it takes at least a week for the vaccine to create sufficient plague antibodies. Like smallpox, mumps, and measles vaccines, the plague vaccine must be given *before* the patient contracts the disease to ward it off. Anyone bitten by a flea infected with *Yersinia pestis*, unless previously inoculated, will writhe in excruciating pain and likely die before the plague antibodies kick in. The currently available vaccine is therefore useless during a fast-spreading epidemic.

Knowing this, Larry surveyed the battlefield like a General George Patton, confident of victory, and the humanlike expression on his face gloated with delight.

His rats swarmed from their caves, hollow dead logs, sewers, and dens and mauled two hundred people on their way, infecting them all with the black death. More than a million strong, they headed to the city's downtown, where they joined up with another quarter million that lived in dens in Willow Park and along the canal.

Larry's plan to infect the city's humans with *Yersinia pestis* would launch his war against human beings worldwide. The fleas on the rats would infest dogs, cats, livestock, and any other creatures on which they could survive. These animals would be flown or sailed overseas on the thousands of planes and ships that crisscrossed the planet daily, and soon the fleas these animals carried would infect several hundred million humans everywhere on the planet.

The one million two hundred fifty thousand rats gathered at bus stops, train stations, and parking lots at exactly ten minutes before five o'clock in the evening, eagerly awaiting the humans who were almost finished at work. Before people could reach their transportation and begin their commutes home, thousands would be savaged. Mayor Perkins had issued as many protective suits as he could lay hands on, but there were enough for just one out of every five hundred people. The majority of the population were sitting ducks, totally defenseless.

Sirens sounded. Dozens of police cars and emergency vehicles plied the streets and over loudspeakers issued this warning: "This is an emergency. This is not a drill. You are in grave danger. Get indoors at once!" Only some heeded the warning and rushed back to their offices. Most tried to make it to their cars, buses, or trains, but nine thousand of these were cut down in the process, the rats tearing chunks of their flesh away like piranha. The assault lasted thirty minutes, until finally the rats retreated.

Larry was pleased. Of the nine thousand who had been cut down, a quarter died within half an hour. The survivors lay writhing in a pain much worse than anything they'd ever known. Soon, those survivors would develop plague symptoms and writhe in torment some more. The rats would attack again the next day, then again the next, and keep attacking until not a soul was left.

*

Mayor Perkins, Tom Garret, Bob Morris, the CDC director, and the governor's chief of staff watched the entire scene unfold on closed-circuit TV. They were in the headquarters building of the city's Department of Transportation, which had cameras mounted at intersections throughout town. "Jesus, God, help us!" Mayor Perkins moaned. "Why did I wait? I should have closed down everything yesterday. I could have declared a state of emergency and ordered everyone to stay at home."

"Based on what we knew, sir, I think you made the best call you could," Garret said. "If you'd announced that a rat army was about to attack, people would have thought you'd gone mad. In our wildest dreams, none of us expected this."

The mayor, however, sensed the true extent of the horror that was taking place, whereas the others, dumbfounded and in disbelief, still couldn't accept it. The plague, Perkins knew, which Larry made sure was a virulent strain, was spreading.

The governor was on the line. "Mr. Mayor, I've been watching the closed-circuit feed too. You have my full support. No way you or any of us could have known this would happen. I'm sending one hundred fifty state troopers and five hundred national guardsmen to supplement your police. They'll arrive midday tomorrow."

"Thank you, Governor. I needed that; I need your support. But it's worse than you think. Much worse! I have CDC Director Mike Friedman here. He wants to speak to you."

"Governor, my people have run tests on several of the victims," Friedman said into the speakerphone. "I received the results a couple of minutes ago. Are you sitting down? All of them are showing signs of a disease that hasn't been around since the late Middle Ages."

"What are you talking about? What disease?"

"Sir, it's incredible," Friedman said, "but they've come down with the bubonic plague, the black death. And this strain is fast moving. People bitten just hours ago are showing advanced symptoms. I don't want to step on your toes, Governor, but I'm calling the president."

The governor, unable to process what he was being told, mumbled, "The black dea ... death?"

"Yes! And those troopers and guardsmen you want to send? Forget it! They'll be attacked and infected too. But the army, marines, and navy seals have thousands of protective suits and oxygen masks stored away. The Centers for Disease Control have thousands as well. We need a regiment of soldiers in here wearing them to take control of the streets. In the meantime, set up blockades on all the main roads. This is not a local emergency; it's national. No one is to leave or enter this zone until the president orders otherwise."

From his skyscraper perch, Larry was listening. *That's their plan? A blockade?* He snickered. *It would take a week for the military to get its equipment together, and by then half the city would be dead.* The war had just started, yet already he could see mangled human bodies littering the streets. Before retreating, his rat army had devoured most of their organs and flesh. Stray dogs joined in. Swarms of flies descended. Crows and turkey vultures tore away slivers, and mice, moles, and squirrels excitedly nibbled away.

The first soldiers began arriving two days later. Another thousand people had been bitten, even though they'd locked themselves in their homes and barricaded the windows and doors. And nothing could keep out the *Yersinia pestis* fleas, which were able to enter through the tiniest of openings. These soldiers, although battle-hardened, having served tours of duty in Afghanistan or Iraq, were mostly kids, with 90 percent of them, not counting the officers, being no older than twenty-three. When Mayor Perkins saw them, his heart sank. There were just three hundred, not even a full battalion, and only half were fully suited with protective gear.

Mayor Perkins was an intelligent and caring leader. He was in the last year of his third term, and most considered him the best mayor in the city's history. He had rooted out corruption, revived the local economy, and delivered city services more effectively than any mayor before him. He was honest and had a beautiful, charismatic wife and three wonderful children. People loved him. He was admired by everyone, but nothing could have prepared him for the catastrophe that was currently unfolding. While he helplessly watched, his neighbors suffered. He'd never be able to forgive himself for failing to protect them.

Perkins and many of the city's top officials were licensed to carry firearms. When his aides told him that his youngest daughter had been among the victims and horribly mauled, they were forced to lock him in his office because he wanted to rush outside with his gun, fight his way home, and kill as many rats as he could on the way. Alone, sitting at his desk, he felt the depth of the tragedy that was currently happening. "My daughter? My neighbors? If only I had acted sooner," he mumbled, "I could have saved them." The horrifying symptoms of bubonic plague had been described to him. First, huge tumors known as *buboes* appeared on the groin, neck, and armpits, oozing pus, bleeding, and often growing as large as lemons. From those body parts, they spread in all directions, accompanied by acute fever and vomiting. Finally, as the infection invaded the lungs and organs, and the victim could no longer breathe, the buboes transformed into large black spots: the black death. That's what Perkins's daughter, he knew, was going through now.

And that evening, trapped in his office with no hope of persuading his aides to let him leave, Mayor Perkins called his family, particularly his dying daughter, to say goodbye, and a minute later he put the barrel of his .40 caliber Beretta 92FS in his mouth and squeezed the trigger.

Chapter 30

John Perkins should not have taken his life so impetuously. The next morning Bob Morris unlocked the mayor's door and he and Tom Garret strode in, excited to tell Perkins some unexpectedly good news: Aubrey Adams's prescient statement that Larry's aura was causing the rats to attack had been disturbingly correct. And so was her statement that R-Five, using the presence, was fighting back, preventing Larry from fully unleashing his powers. But instead of getting to deliver this good news, they were confronted with Perkins's blood-spattered body slumped on his desk facedown. Initially, the impact of the bullet had thrown him forcefully against the seatback of his rolling chair, and then the rear wheels swiveled sharply ninety degrees, the sudden jolt ricocheting him forward. Like everybody else, Morris and Garret loved Perkins; they both rushed to his side, hoping for a pulse. A large pool of blood, however, had collected on the desk's glass top, and brain tissue was protruding through a gaping wound in his head. They found a suicide note next to him, which read simply, "To my beloved family and my wonderful constituents and friends, forgive me."

The news Morris and Garret would have told him, although encouraging, was only partially good. R-Five could not save those who had already been infected by the *Yersinia pestis* fleas, including the mayor's daughter. But beginning last night, just before Perkins had shot himself, R-Five had been able to disinfect them to such an extent that they were no longer able to spread the black death. Larry's rat army, however, was still wholly intact and savage as ever. The few people who were foolish enough to venture outside were set upon and literally eaten alive.

Actually, R-Five hadn't disinfected the *Yersinia pestis* fleas but had forced Larry to, because only Larry's aura could alter the physiology of living things. The huge burst of energy R-Five had used to force the aura to disinfect them, however, enabled Larry to regain his fix on the location of the presence. He'd felt the presence penetrating deep into his head as it neutralized his aura's power.

Unlike Larry, however, none of the people in attendance at Mayor Perkins's meeting had lost their fix on the presence because R-Five hadn't prevented them from retaining the knowledge that it was emanating from him. R-Five wanted them to keep their fix and know that he was the only thing stopping the aura from annihilating the human race.

So, everything was now out in the open. Tom Garret, Bob Morris, Aubrey, Becky, the governor's chief of staff, the CDC director, and the Republican and Democratic leaders of the city council all knew that R-Five was involved in the epic struggle that was unfolding. And that the struggle was epic, and that Larry and R-Five's powers were real, not even Republican leader Peters doubted any longer.

*

The presence, like the aura, has a number of incredible capabilities but they are not the same. First off, unlike the aura, the presence is not proactive, but reactive. That is, it self-adjusts, and R-Five is unable to ratchet its strength up any more than exactly the amount needed to counter the strength of the aura. Like PRT, which always self-adjusted just enough to metabolize whatever quantity of carbohydrates a *Rattus norvegicus diabetica* consumed, the presence does only what is necessary.

Second, the presence, into which the PRT had morphed within R-Five, is a separate, sentient being over which R-Five does not have full control. Their relationship is symbiotic; R-Five needs the presence to prevent Larry from slaughtering everyone, and the presence needs R-Five's body to survive.

Third, the most incredible thing about the presence is that it exists not only in our dimension but also in others simultaneously. Until Einstein came along, scientists believed there were only three dimensions: height, width, and length. Einstein's theory of relativity, however, gave rise to a four-dimensional concept that included time, which is a dimension of duration, unlike the other three, which are spatial. Einstein's concept is called the "space-time continuum." But the presence does not have just four dimensions, it has five. That is, it can move up and down (the dimension of height) and from side to side (the dimensions of width and length); it has duration (the dimension of time); and it can also move into another dimension, the fifth dimension.

Most people have difficulty understanding the only four-dimensional space-time concept Einstein came up with. Picturing physical reality as five-dimensional is more difficult still, but the mental gymnastics necessary are not beyond the ability of any person willing to use his or her imagination and try.

Einstein's illustration of space-time is a sheet of rubber that can expand, contract, curl, or lie flat to accommodate displacement by planets, stars, nebulae, and other celestial bodies. The rubber sheet has duration, and for it, time passes just as it does for all of us. In trying to locate yourself within this illustration, think of the rubber sheet as having boundaries—a top, a bottom, and sides—with a hollow space in between, like the space inside a tire inner tube. Think of that tire inner tube space as the place where we all live and that contains the entire known physical universe. This tire inner tube space of only four dimensions is a bounded universe of perception, but not a bounded universe in reality. If you picture this hollow space with small people running around, you'll have an idea of not only what four-dimensional space-time feels like to people inside that space but also what this same space-time might look like to someone outside it.

To us inhabitants of the tire inner tube, time passes, and movement in all directions is possible until we hit the boundary of the tube, which is the boundary of our reality. To us, this tire inner tube universe is all that exists. The tire inner tube's boundary is not a real boundary, but merely the boundary of our mind's ability to perceive. However, since this is the only universe that we inhabitants of the tube know, we believe ourselves to be free to move in all directions. We do not perceive the boundary. But from the perspective of someone outside the tire inner tube, life and movement inside it is very limited. We inhabitants sealed within the inner tube are unaware that there is anything beyond the tube.

But what is beyond it? Or, to put the same question differently, where is this someone outside the tire inner tube watching from?

To someone outside the four-dimensional tube, it appears that the entire tube we four-dimensional creatures live in exists within another, larger tire inner tube, a layer that contains the smaller layer and is five-dimensional rather than four. Moreover, this five-dimensional layer exists within other layers that are of dimensions even higher in number. Each of the layers shaped like a tire inner tube is contained within a higher-dimensional, more inclusive layer. Each layer penetrates the layers within it yet is not perceived as doing so by the inhabitants of the lower-dimensional tubes, since for them their lower-dimensional tube is all that exists and all they can see and feel.

Within the four-dimensional layer—our layer—we are at a particular place in physical space at a particular time. But in five-dimensional and higher-dimensional layers, *we can be at different places at the same time.* Someone watching the four-dimensional tire inner tube from the fifth-dimensional tube is in both layers at the same time.

To better understand this, imagine a world of just two dimensions, length and width, but with no height, populated by two-dimensional creatures that can move forward and backward, and from left to right and vice versa, but not up. They can't perceive *up* or even conceive the concept of *up*. Now imagine yourself standing on that world like on a flat piece of paper. Because you're spatially three-dimensional, you can move forward, backward, from side to side, and also up. You have no difficulty perceiving *up* because it is something natural and part of what you experience every day. You're in the two-dimensional world and the three-dimensional world at the same time. You are, in fact, in two places at the same time.

Now imagine you're standing on the same two-dimensional flat-piece-of-paper world but that your feet have penetrated the paper so that the lower half of your body is below the flat-piece-of-paper world and the upper half of your body is above it. Not only are the two-dimensional creatures unable to perceive *up*, but also they are unable to perceive *down*. You, however, are in the two-dimensional world and above and below it at the same time. You are, in fact, now in three places at the same time.

Also, think of what happens when you daydream. In your daydreams, you can do things that are not normally possible. You can see the same thing from different perspectives. You can see the left side and right side and the top and the bottom of an object all at once, and you can be in many different places all at once. Daydreaming serves as an approximation of what movement for someone in the fifth dimension and higher dimensions is like.

If you're still confused (and if you aren't, you're another Einstein), remember the questions we used to ask when we were kids. "Mom, Dad, does space go on forever? Doesn't it end somewhere? And where it ends, what's beyond that?" The answer is this: In the four-dimensional universe shaped like a tire inner tube that we live in, space ends at the boundary of our perception, that is, at the boundary of our inner tube layer. But since we are unable to detect that boundary because of our limited understanding of the physical universe, our senses tell us that no boundary exists. That's why when we look at the night sky and can't see or imagine where it ends—its boundary—we feel that space must go on and on forever. It does not. What's beyond the limit of our perception, that is, beyond the boundary of our limited four-dimensional tire inner tube layer, is the fifth dimension (and beyond that, the sixth dimension, the seventh dimension, and higher dimensions), and that's where someone outside our layer is watching from.

The fifth dimension is from where the presence had been watching everything.

Chapter 31

To supplement the three-hundred-man regiment that the president had sent to Burlington the day before Perkins shot himself, a heavily armed second contingent arrived. They were three battalions, mostly special ops, all carrying tribeam laser rifles and wearing full-body hazmat suits. Their orders were to attack Larry's army of rats immediately and kill as many as possible. Tribeam laser rifles have no lower barrel, so when they're fired, the beam is not focused and spreads wide, incinerating everything within a several-yard radius. Even with this lethal weaponry, however, the three special ops battalions were unable to turn the tide and could only barely slow the rampaging army of rats.

To compensate for the presence's having neutralized his *Yersinia pestis* fleas, Larry used his aura to summon a million rats from neighboring towns to reinforce his army. The rats now outnumbered the humans forty to one. You'd think the humans would barricade themselves indoors, but many households were running low on food and people were forced to venture out to replenish provisions.

The governor imposed martial law. Newscasters on every radio station and TV channel repeatedly announced, "Citizens, you are not to leave your homes. If you do, for your own protection, you'll be arrested and detained in the Main Street armory." These warnings were being broadcast every five minutes on all local airwaves.

They enraged Larry because, with R-Five's having prevented him from spreading the plague and with the humans having been ordered to stay indoors, he could no longer slaughter thousands in the street in a single attack. He could now count on killing only a few dozen a day, when the rats were able to enter poorly rodent-protected homes.

He changed his tactics. Using his aura, Larry set about causing the already formidable teeth and claws of the rats to grow longer, sharper, and stronger. Soon, hordes of them would be able to gnaw and claw their way in through the wooden doors and sides of even well-shielded houses.

Before Larry could finish altering their physiology, however, and put this new plan into full effect, R-Five powerfully hurled the presence at him. Larry could feel it penetrating his head, causing intense pain again, as it fought to counter his aura. His rat army managed to kill only fifty people before the pain forced him to back down and cause the rats' teeth and claws to resume exactly the same size and shape as before.

"Why are you helping them, damn you? You're a fool for protecting them."

"Does that in ... include Au ... Aubrey and Be ... Becky? Does it include Do ... Doctor Ga ... Gary Schwartz and the en ... energy he ... healers who sa ... saved us?"

R-Five and Larry were communicating telepathically. The aura and presence enabled them to.

"It includes all humans. You remember how they imprisoned us in that stinking little cage, the endless insulin shots, and their difethialone and indandione poisons, don't you?"

"I reme ... remember everything, La ... Larry, but you ... you've gone mad."

"Have I, R-Five? I think it's you who's gone mad. Join me instead of fighting me, and we'll kill all of them in a week."

"No, La ... Larry. I won't al ... allow that. Be ... besides, you don't just want to kill them, you want to tor ... torture them. And by the way, you should stop call ... calling me R-Five all the time."

"What? Then what should I call you? Traitor?"

"Fu ... funny, Larry. But when I'm here, n ... near you, a more ac ... accurate name would be *Feras indomitus 5*. There's a reason why he stu ... stutters like me and re ... reminds you so much of me. There's a rea ... reason why when you're with him you alm ... almost feel like you're with me."

"I do feel that way, R-Five, but what the hell are you talking about?"

"With your inte … intellect, La … Larry, I'm sur … surprised you haven't fig … figured it out yet. Espe … especially af … after I see … seemingly disa … disappeared and *Feras indomitus 5* seemingly took my place."

He was right. Until now, Larry hadn't spoken to, seen, heard from, or sensed R-Five for nearly a year. During that time, only when *Rattus feras indomitus 5* was around could he feel happy and at ease.

"Sometimes, R-Five, I suspect that *Rattus feras indomitus 5* is you in disguise."

"You've al … almost got it. Ex … except *Rattus feras indomitus 5* isn't me in disguise but is me and him at the same time. You see, La … Larry, the presence en … enables me to be in two p … places at the same time."

Larry's jaw dropped. He was stunned. "That's not possible."

"But it is. Larry, *Rattus feras indomitus 5* is me in the fourth dim … dimension, and R-Five is me in the fifth. That's why I, as R-Five, was ab … able to be in Cal … Calcutta with you and why I, as *Rattus feras indomitus 5*, was a … able to be here in Burl … Burlington with Three, Four, and the others at the same time."

"I still don't get you."

"Th … think abo … about it. You can read the mi … mind of any liv … living thing, but you ca … can't read mine. Why do you think that is?"

Now Larry began to stutter. "I … I'm not sure, R-Five."

"It's be … because you can't enter the fifth dimension. It's be … beyond the li … limit of your per … perception. When I'm there as R-Five, my thoughts are beyond your reach."

"What do you mean?"

"I mean that for you, this four-dimen … dimensional world is all there is. Eve … even when you went to oth … other ga … galaxies, you were still tra ... trapped in this li ... limited layer. But I'm not only in this w ... world; I'm in the fifth-dim ... dimensional world at the same time. I can read your mind whe ... whenever I want to, but you can ne ... never read m ... mine unless I let you."

"If that's true, then how come I can't read *Rattus feras indomitus 5*'s mind? You just said that he's you when you're in the fourth dimension. And since I can read the minds of every living thing here, I should be able to read his."

"It's be ... because he and I are the same, Larry. R-Five and *Rattus feras indomitus 5* are one. I'm in the fourth-dim ... dimensional world and, by using the presence, am in the fifth-dim ... dimensional world at the same time. I keep my thoughts hi ... hidden in the fifth dimension and allow them to en ... enter the fourth only when I want them to. *Rattus feras indomitus 5* is only the limited four-dim ... dimensional part of me that you can see and talk to with your lim ... limited four-dimen ... dimensional per ... perception of reality."

"Why are you telling me this? You've given away your secret, fool."

"I'm tel ... telling you be ... because there's no ... nothing you can do about it. I'm hoping I can per ... persuade you to stop your insanity so I won't have to injure you. Your aura can't de ... defeat me, I will not let you torture the hu ... humans. But if you per ... persist, I guar ... guarantee I'll torture you."

Larry, although stunned by this revelation, almost laughed and was unafraid because he knew R-Five's threat meant nothing. It only caused his contempt for his former and once dear cage-mate to grow deeper. There was another secret about the presence, a weakness that R-Five hadn't revealed but that Larry could plainly sense. His lizard-like tongue slithered in and out. He hadn't quite put his finger on it yet, but he undoubtedly soon would.

Chapter 32

The gray matter in the reptilian portion of Larry's brain had grown terrifyingly massive. There was now more of it there than in his cerebral cortex. His eyes were cold, unblinking slits.

His split slimy tongue, like some lizards' and all snakes', could taste organic molecules drifting through the air. It tasted lethal *E. coli* bacteria, which Larry decided to use to infect the humans, whom he'd come to look upon as *prey*.

Very slowly and gently, so his aura would not attract the attention of the presence, Larry caused bacteria in the city's reservoir to reproduce abnormally and multiply exponentially. Most bacteria are harmless, but a few strains, such as *E. coli O157:H7*, produce powerful toxins that can cause high fever, bloody diarrhea, and kidney failure. The currently available antibiotics are often ineffective, so once *E. coli* takes hold in an individual whose immune system is unable to naturally fight it off, advanced symptoms and death frequently followed.

E. coli comes from human and animal feces, and during rainfalls and snowmelts, unsafe quantities are sometimes washed into streams, rivers, and lakes that are used as sources of drinking water. Before such water enters public drinking systems, it's usually collected in reservoirs, where treatment with chlorine or other chemicals inactivates deadly microorganisms. Inadequately treated water can cause lethal outbreaks. In Ontario, Canada, in spring 2000, *E. coli O157:H7* killed seven people, mostly children, and infected thousands who drank the contaminated water. More recently, in Germany, in summer 2011, forty-five people died and five thousand were infected by a similar *E. coli* strain, but this time from eating contaminated food. The point is that *E. coli* infection can be extraordinarily deadly, is often untreatable, and ranks up there with legionnaire's disease and anthrax.

Water containing a concentration of more than 5 percent *E. coli* per liter is potentially toxic, but Larry had managed to quadruple that amount in the city's reservoir without being detected by the presence.

The sharp increase had not been detected by the public authorities either. Although they usually tested samples from the reservoir two times a month, the rampaging rat army, which assaulted anyone who ventured outside, prevented that from happening. Within less than a week, the water contaminated with *E. coli* was being piped into every home and business throughout the city, and before R-Five realized what was happening and could react, fifty thousand people became ill and seven thousand died from it.

*

From his observation point on the high terrace where he was monitoring his war against people, Larry cast his aura and found that R-Five, at least the four-dimensional part of him, Feras 5, was back in his stinking little cage at the UVM laboratory with *Rattus norvegicus diabetica 1–4*.

One, Two, Three, and Four could no longer speak. In fact, they could barely think. With Larry's having been gone for a year and therefore not constantly bathing them in his aura, the gray matter of their brains had reverted to its former ridiculously small, but normal for rats, size. He focused his attention only on R-Five, who he now knew was one and the same as Feras 5, challenging him.

Communicating telepathically, Larry said, "You shouldn't make threats unless you can carry them out. I'm onto you."

"Don't p ... push it, L ... Larry. I've been ho ... holding myself back, but if you m ... murder humans again, the p ... pain you've felt so far will be like a pinprick in com ... comparison."

"I think not, my friend. I think your presence can't do anything except react just enough to counteract my aura, because if you could have, you would have killed me by now."

That comment wiped the usual amused smile off R-Five's face. Suddenly, a strange sensation he'd never felt before rose up in him. It was more than concern and more than worry, but not quite terror. It was dread.

"I've got your vulnerability figured out, R-Five. The reason you haven't killed me is because you can't."

Immediately, R-Five shifted most of his thoughts into the fifth dimension to shield them from the aura.

"That won't work, Five. I don't have to read your mind to know that the presence can never adjust its strength upward any more than the exact amount required to counter my aura. I know this because I was injected with Professor Tompkins's self-adjusting insulin too, which never adjusted to a dose any higher than the exact amount required to metabolize whatever quantity of carbohydrates we had eaten. The more carbohydrates, the more it adjusted; the fewer carbohydrates, the less it adjusted. That's how the PRT kept our diabetes under control, and that's how you've been using your presence to keep me under control."

Hearing that, R-Five hesitated, uncertain what to do or say. *Unfortunately,* he thought, *Larry is right.* And Larry was right, except for one important detail: although the presence couldn't adjust upward more than to the exact level necessary to control Larry's aura, in order to find that level, it often over adjusted for a few moments before sinking down to the aura's level. During those moments, R-Five had the advantage and was considerably more powerful.

Larry decided to attack, unable to restrain the reptilian portion of his brain, and with his frightening forked tongue slithering in and out.

But before his aura could land a single a blow, R-Five hurled the presence at him. Since it came at him from the fifth dimension, Larry, with his limited four-dimensional perception of reality, failed to see it coming and was knocked from his high skyscraper perch. He plummeted toward the ground, but halfway down, in midair, he managed to disassemble himself and, molecule by molecule, cast himself atop the table where his old little cage sat, and then reassemble into his six-inch body.

R-Five exited the cage. As his presence receded to exactly the aura's level, he and Larry charged each other. Face-to-face, with their limbs entwined like wrestlers, they struggled to a draw, totally exhausted.

*

Suddenly, Aubrey arrived. She walked straight to the table's edge and stood there motionless, towering over them. Anger contorted her face. The aura and the presence had no effect on her. She slammed her right fist hard on the table, which, as she had intended, pried Larry and R-Five apart. Then, in a rage, taking them by surprise, she swatted them both so forcefully that Larry's right front femur, tibia, and ankle and R-Five's left front femur, tibia, and ankle snapped and shattered.

They were both gravely injured, their comminuted broken bones protruding through the skin. Blood spurted from their mouths, their noses, and the hideous wounds on their legs. They were lucky they were still alive.

PART VII

AUBREY

Chapter 33

Aubrey was born near Burlington, Vermont, one of the most beautiful cities in the country. If it weren't for its long, cold winters, Burlington's population, including university students and suburb dwellers, would be much larger than a mere hundred thousand people. Fortunately for the city's residents, the cold weather deterred hordes of people from moving there and protected it from becoming just another nondescript, paved-over, and much too crowded metropolis. Nearly every survey taken during the past twenty years ranked Burlington among the top ten best places to live in the United States.

The landscape surrounding the city is breathtaking. On the west side, separating Vermont from New York, is the one-hundred-twenty-five-mile long and, on average, nearly two-mile-wide Lake Champlain, which extends north into Canada and south all the way to Ticonderoga on the New York side of the Vermont-New York border. To the north, east, and south of Burlington are woods and forests, dozens of villages and hamlets, and many mountains, which are home to some of the best skiing in the United States, including Sugarbush, Stowe, Jay Peak, and Smugglers' Notch. Vermont is not only a winter wonderland but also a warm weather paradise, and during spring and summer the opportunities for canoeing, sailing, camping, hiking, and viewing wildlife are endless. Bear, moose, coyote, white-tailed deer, bobcats, eagles, and hawks are everywhere, and encounters with them are frequent. Wolves, lynx, and even cougars are also occasionally spotted.

Aubrey grew up twenty miles northeast of Burlington on a chicken farm in the town of Westford. It was there that she learned to care for a multitude of different animals because her parents bred horses and raised geese, turkey, pigs, goats, some sheep, and a few milk cows. By the time she was thirteen, she'd assisted the local veterinarians in treating so many farm animal ailments and in delivering so many foals, lambs, kids, and calves that she could do it herself if necessary.

You've heard of horse whispering, which is practiced by people who can read the body language and sense the thoughts of horses. It all started with a man from Groveport, Ohio, named John Solomon Rarey, who lived in the mid-1800s and tamed his first horse at the age of twelve. To gain their confidence, he invented a technique that gained him international fame, repeatedly using it to tame the most malevolent, highly traumatized horses in the world.

The specific technique Rarey used, which he wrote about in his book *The Complete Horse Tamer*, published in 1862, consisted of hobbling one of the horse's legs with a strap, which enabled him to quickly control the animal and tire it out. He then made the horse lie down and gently stroked it until the horse was convinced, in the most peaceful way possible, that Rarey was its master. The technique was so effective that he was even able to tame zebras so they could be ridden like the most docile of horses.

Word of his gift spread, and in 1858 he was summoned to Windsor Castle in England to calm a ferocious horse owned by Queen Victoria. The queen watched, astonished, as Rarey put his hands on the animal, laid it on the ground before her, and rested his head on its hooves. Within minutes he brought it completely under control.

But Aubrey's rapport with animals surpassed even Rarey's. While she was still in junior high school, she developed her whispering ability to such an extent that she could whisper, not just with horses, but with every animal on her family's farm, including the chickens, turkeys, and geese.

A larger animal like a horse or cow, especially one in pain from an illness or injury, could easily have harmed Aubrey, but never in all the years she ministered to them had that happened. There were two or three other skilled whisperers in the area, but Aubrey was the one the local veterinarians regularly called upon to help treat difficult animals when their own efforts had failed. It was remarkable that she had so much success with large farm mammals, but more remarkable still was that she could also effectively whisper with the chickens and other poultry birds. She was often able to cure them too. The key to her success was not that she could somehow magically cure illnesses or mend broken bones, but that she could almost always gain the animals' trust and, by doing so, calm them to such an extent that their natural immune responses and healing processes kicked in. Also, when the animals were calm, the medications administered by the vets usually became more effective.

She was so good at whispering that her reputation spread throughout Burlington and then Vermont, soon spreading across the entire Northeast and beyond. A couple of times she was even flown out to a ranch in Wyoming by a wealthy horse breeder who was worried that his most prolific and profitable stallion was becoming too ill to mate from a rare strain of Potomac horse fever. She couldn't totally cure the fever but was able to extend the stallion's life many years beyond when he otherwise would have died.

A difference between Rarey's and Aubrey's whispering was that his remained strong and steady till the day he passed away, whereas hers, much stronger than his to begin with, noticeably dissipated when she became a lab animal technician. Aubrey, now responsible for the care of the thousands of animals in a large lab animal colony, often focused her whispering on many animals simultaneously to relieve their ailments. That shift in focus from one animal to many spread her whispering wide, over an entire colony sometimes, and reduced its effectiveness.

But saying Aubrey's whispering ability had become less effective would be like saying that Diana Nyad could no longer swim once she was older. In 2013, after four previous failed attempts, Nyad finally swam the one hundred ten miles of open ocean from Florida to Cuba. She did it nonstop in two days and five hours. She was sixty-four.

Obviously, like Diana, Aubrey's extraordinary talent was still potent. That she had used it to overcome Larry's aura and Five's presence, however, and grievously injure them haunted her.

*

Larry and R-Five lay critically wounded and writhing in exquisite pain. Even if Aubrey was so inclined, which she definitely was not, no amount of whispering could heal them from the injuries she'd inflicted.

Chapter 34

Aubrey was eleven when her father brought her to Maine, where he had business to take care of and where she met Moxus for the first time. A Penobscot Indian known internationally among Native peoples to be the most talented energy healer in the world, Moxus resided on the Penobscot Tribal Reservation in the northeast corner of the state. According to the 2020 census, the reservation's total population was around seven hundred fifty-eight, but of that small number, an oddly high proportion were skilled healers. They all had been trained by Moxus, his generation's master energy medicine practitioner.

Aubrey's father, on a whim, felt it was time for the world's greatest healer and his daughter, potentially the world's greatest whisperer, to become acquainted. He wanted Moxus to assess the true extent of her abilities.

Moxus had met whisperers before. The moment he laid eyes on Aubrey, he knew she was exceptional. The aura he detected emanating from her, in her case whispering, was unwaveringly steady, remarkably strong, and, what surprised him most, enormously kind. Nonhealers, that is, the vast majority of people not attuned to auras, would have trouble sensing even hers, but animals like cows, horses, chickens, and ducks, and especially wild animals, totally reliant on their natural senses to survive, would have no trouble at all.

In fact, Moxus knew that animals would be reassured by Aubrey's aura, made to feel safe by it, and be totally enveloped in its kindness. That, of course, was her secret.

Aubrey didn't see Moxus again until fourteen years later, when he and the other healers walked into the UVM animal laboratory and began gently waving their hands over Larry and the other *Rattus norvegicus diabetica*.

Before they departed the reservation, Moxus told Aubrey's dad, "To say the least, Mr. Adams, I'm impressed. You should keep an eye on your daughter. There's been no whisperer her equal since John Rarey died in 1866. Your daughter's whispering is so potent that I think she may be capable of healing any living creature from almost anything."

If Mr. Adams had extended their visit just a day longer, he and Aubrey would have met Moxus's next visitors, Dr. Gary Schwartz and Professor Simona Gupta. Holding gently onto Simona's hand was a small sickly child, known then by his birth name, Rohan Karteray. The boy was Gupta's six-year-old son, and she desperately hoped Moxus's powers could heal him.

Chapter 35

They'd crashed heavily to the floor after Aubrey swatted them. Larry was unconscious, and R-Five lay comatose beside him. Their gruesome wounds had bled profusely, but just before Larry passed out, he used his ability to alter the physiology of any living thing to staunch the bleeding.

In his horribly weakened condition, Larry was unable to focus his aura on only himself. Although he detested R-Five, his aura stopped his bleeding too.

An ALAT found them and put them back in their cage. The ALAT reported their condition to Becky, who instructed him to begin intravenous feeding, but if they worsened, to euthanize both. After several hours, revived somewhat from the intravenous nourishment, they regained consciousness, but it was apparent their wounds were so severe that they'd likely die.

Becky thought back to everything that had happened and created a list in her mind of each major event:

- A year ago, 2,860 *Rattus norvegicus diabetica* were delivered to the lab.

- At the time she, Becky, was the manager of Tompkins's experiment, testing those rats with PRT.

- The rats' capillaries started hemorrhaging because of stress.

- Dr. Schwartz brought in energy healers, who successfully stopped their bleeding.

- Larry developed an aura so powerful that he became superintelligent.

- Tompkins's self-adjusting insulin experiment was suddenly stopped and changed to a mere cure-for-baldness experiment.

- Larry took control of Becky's thoughts and forced her to open the latch on his cage door.

- Tompkins's Indian investors and others, including herself, had forgotten his PRT experiment at UVM had ever taken place.

- Larry had become obsessed with his hatred for humans but tried to restrain himself from using his aura to kill them.

- A presence had grown inside R-Five that he used to keep Larry's aura in check.

- Mayor Perkins shot himself when Larry's army of plague-infested rats swarmed from their dens and began slaughtering people.

Becky tried to make sense of it all but couldn't. She wrote each event down, cut the paper into slips with scissors, and moved the slips around, trying, like when doing the word puzzle called SENSE, to come up with a solution. She moved the last event to the front, ESENS, and she moved the middle one to the end, NSESE, but the rearrangements meant nothing. Whatever was going on was beyond her.

Becky recalled other events and added them in:

- She and Bob Morris had known some third force was in play, one more powerful than the aura or presence.

- Aubrey, unlike everyone else, never forgot about Tompkins's PRT experiment at UVM.

But no matter how many events she recalled, she could form no coherent picture.

Totally frustrated, Becky focused her thoughts once more on Larry and R-Five. She still cared deeply about her lab animals and, above all, those two.

She phoned Gary Schwartz in his Tucson office at the Laboratory for Advances in Consciousness and Health. He agreed to take a six o'clock flight to Atlanta the next morning and catch a connecting flight to Burlington, swearing he'd arrive at the UVM animal lab no later than midafternoon.

PART VIII

ROHAN

Chapter 36

As promised, Dr. Schwartz arrived at UVM midday. Becky had asked him there because maybe, once again, he could find a way to save Larry and R-Five, this time not from hemorrhaging capillaries, but from their hideous fractures and wounds. *Maybe*, she thought, *his energy healers can do even that.*

Simona Gupta was expected the same day, having booked a flight from Calcutta. Flying in on a red-eye, she met up with Dr. Schwartz at the Burlington airport. They arrived at the lab together in a rental car.

Upon entering, they immediately walked to cage 28, where they stood, watching.

Larry's fur had lost its luster. His teeth had become dull and yellow, and the humanlike expressions that just days ago often crossed his face could no longer be detected. A smidgen of his intelligence and powerful aura remained, but both were rapidly diminishing. R-Five huddled beside him. His old, blank and dull, rather stupid appearance had returned in full. The once powerful presence within him had all but disappeared. He was trapped, like the rest of us, in a limited four-dimensional world—height, width, length, and time—and his ability to travel into the fifth dimension was totally gone.

Aubrey and Becky were there too, standing near cage 28. Becky was still bewildered by all the inexplicable events that she was trying to piece together. One of those events randomly crossed her mind: *An undetected third force in play more powerful than the aura and presence!*

At once, without Aubrey's saying anything, Becky heard Aubrey's thoughts. *Maybe you and Bob Morris are right about that?*

Startled, Becky stared at her friend. Still not speaking, she thought, *That undetectable force. It's been you, Aubrey, hasn't it, all along?*

"No, Becky, not true! It wasn't me."

"Oh, come on Aub. It had to have been you!"

"What are you talking abou—?"

Aubrey caught herself midthought, realizing she wasn't talking but using her whispering to communicate mentally with Becky. She also realized that Becky had to have realized it too. Aubrey knew, therefore, that there'd be no longer any point in trying to conceal her ability from her dearest of friends. She wasn't defensive but relieved. At last, she could confide in her.

They were several feet behind Gupta and Schwartz and far enough away to be out of earshot. No longer just thinking, but speaking aloud, Aubrey said, "Yes, Becky, you're right. I have been influencing things, but only to an extent. My whispering, like the aura and the presence, enables me to sometimes sense and control the thoughts of not just horses, but all living things. I've always been able to sense yours, Beck. For a while, by using my whispering, I was able to prevent Five and Larry from destroying each other and our whole damn planet."

"What do you mean, only to an extent? Wasn't it you who made everyone forget Tompkins's insulin experiment and suddenly changed it to baldness medication tests? Wasn't it you who stopped Larry from exterminating the human race? For a while I thought it might be Moxus, but whatever incredible abilities he once possessed dissipated long ago."

"Yes, Becky. I also thought it might be Moxus, but he's ninety-eight years old and in a Maine nursing home now, too feeble to even feed himself. But I had nothing to do with making everyone forget Professor Tompkins's experiment. Whatever did somehow didn't affect me, because I remembered every detail. The most I accomplished with my whispering was to sometimes keep Larry's aura and Five's presence in check. And I admit I'm the one—I regret it now—who severely injured Larry and R-Five. But stopping them from destroying everything? No! When I attacked them, it was if something was controlling me and forcing me to."

"Then what the hell is going on, Aubrey? If it wasn't you, then who or what stopped Larry and Five and made everyone forget?"

"I think I know. Uh, do you remember the night Mayor Perkins killed himself?"

"Of course I do. We heard the shot. You and I were downstairs from his office when it happened."

"Yes, every person in the building heard it, but at the time you thought the shot came from outside, a stray bullet fired in the street by someone shooting at the rats. Everyone thought that except me, Beck. Something prevented you from realizing Perkins was committing suicide. I tried to stop him but couldn't. My whispering was overpowered. I think Perkins was about to order that the third-generation poisons be released to slaughter all the rats. Whatever stopped me from saving him didn't want that."

"You're right, I did think the shot came from the street. But the only thing that makes sense is that Larry stopped you from saving the mayor so he couldn't issue the order to use the new poisons. Larry wanted the rats alive so they'd keep killing people."

"No, Beck, I'm sure it wasn't him, because I used my whispering to read Larry's mind. Although he wanted to kill Perkins, he couldn't because his aura was overpowered. My whispering has difficulty reading R-Five's thoughts, but I picked up enough to know that it wasn't him either. He wanted the poisons released so that Larry's rat army would die and be unable to slaughter people."

"So, Aubrey, where does that leave us?"

"Well, I've been thinking: how well do you know Simona Gupta?"

"What's she got to do with any of this?"

"Did you know she has a son and he's diabetic, Becky?"

"No, I don't know anything about her personal life. She's my boss, and yours, but I've never socialized with her."

"Well, after I comprehended that neither the aura nor the presence was controlling things, it occurred to me, as it occurred to you, that another, more potent force was responsible. As I've told you, it wasn't my whispering, so I decided to check the personnel files of every person who ever worked at our lab in connection with Professor Tompkins's research."

"And you found something?"

"Yes. I learned that Professor Gupta has published more scientific papers and conducted more experiments related to diabetes than any other researcher in the world. Far, far more experiments! She's a near fanatic. She's driven."

"So?"

"I wanted to understand why she's so driven. She's tried so many experiments to discover a cure, some of which were so dangerous that they were lethal to her test subject apes. It's like she's way beyond driven—she's desperate."

"So?" Becky said again.

"Well, it turns out that her son's got a very rare and very destructive variant of type 1 diabetes. While still in her womb, her boy had kidney failure and the doctors had to force premature birth. He was a four-month-old fetus barely breathing and in cardiac arrest, but he survived."

"Where are you going with this, Aubrey?"

"When I found that out, I knew I was onto something, and I'm positive that Gupta's experiments in Calcutta are what kept her son alive. One of the medications she discovered, although it didn't work on diabetics with the usual forms of type 1 or 2, worked on him. It wasn't a total cure, but it managed to slow the destruction of his organs and keep him from dying. He wasn't totally cured until he turned twenty and she tried Tompkins's PRT on him."

"My God, I didn't know there was any human testing. I'm listening, Aubrey."

"She didn't just make sure he took four small PRT injections per day like Tompkins instructed us to give the rats. She made sure he took ten massive injections of it daily. The injections worked and eliminated his diabetes, but with even stranger side effects than the rats'. The side effect for Larry was his aura, and the side effect for R-Five was the presence. But here's the kicker: the side effects for Gupta's son, although similar, are off-the-charts more powerful."

"Wait! Are you telling me that it was him who stopped you from preventing Perkins's suicide and made you attack Larry and Five?"

"That's exactly what I'm telling you. Gupta's son was giving himself such huge and such frequent shots of PRT that it became a force colossally more powerful than Five's presence, Larry's aura, and my whispering combined."

"Jesus! And it was him who somehow made everyone forget Tompkins's PRT experiment?"

"Yes, I'm sure of it."

"Are you serious? Who the hell is her son anyhow?"

*

Several ALATs walked over to where Simona and Gary Schwartz were standing. The tallest warmly hugged Simona, and she hugged him back. She kissed him on the cheek and stroked his hair.

"You look wonderful. I've never seen you looking so healthy."

"Thanks, Mom. I missed you a lot."

"Not as much as I missed you, Rohan."

The last time Rohan had visited Moxus was just before the ninety-eight-year-old Penobscot Indian became so weak that he was moved into a nursing home. The first time was when Rohan was age six, when his mom took him to Maine, hoping that the great energy healer could cure his diabetes. Rohan Karteray had been visiting Moxus regularly ever since.

159

"I'm taking you out to dinner later, Mom. And I'm paying."

"No way, Rohan. I always pay, and that's that."

"Not this time, Mom. I insist. And around here, remember, people don't call me Rohan."

"All right, have it your way. It'll be hard to get used to, but from now on I'll force myself to use your American name. From now on, I promise, I'll call you Ron Carter!"

Chapter 37

"No, sir, that wasn't on Ron Carter's health form when he applied for the ALAT job. He didn't write he had diabetes; he wrote he was recovering from leukemia." Becky Byers was addressing the US attorney general, who was polite but intimidating as he leaned toward her attentively in his high-backed black leather chair.

"Still, Miss Byers, how could you have overlooked his obvious symptoms for so long?"

"Because, Mr. Attorney General," she answered, "the physical examination required for Carter to work in our lab was done in Calcutta by Simona Gupta, his mother! She signed off on him. I didn't know he was her son. She falsified his medical report. It specifically said he had leukemia—in remission."

Becky Byers had been subpoenaed by the Justice Department to their headquarters in Washington, DC. Around an ultraglossy teakwood conference table, in addition to Becky, sat Dr. Schwartz and Professor Tompkins, both of whom had also been subpoenaed; CDC Director Mike Friedman; the Republican and Democratic leaders of the Burlington City Council; Burlington's acting mayor, Bob Morris, who'd been appointed by the council to replace John Perkins until new elections could be held; and the attorney general himself. Neither Schwartz, Tompkins, nor Byers had hired attorneys because they'd all been granted immunity. Gupta and her son, defying their subpoenas, were not in attendance.

"I hear you, Miss Byers, but didn't it strike you as odd that so much more PRT was being used than you were injecting into the rats? Are you saying that you and your entire staff never noticed it was being depleted? Didn't you guys ever inventory the stuff?"

"Of course we inventoried it! We did notice and considered all possibilities: that the PRT holding containers were leaking, that it was being siphoned off, or that we somehow overmeasured the amount of PRT we had in stock. We questioned everyone who had access to it but never found evidence that Carter or anyone was stealing it. We had no reason to suspect him of anything."

"Well, why the hell not? Your lab has security cameras monitoring everything. They had to have recorded Carter stealing it and injecting himself with massive doses. Right?"

"Respectfully, sir," Bob Morris said, interrupting, "no! That is, the cameras did record him stealing and injecting PRT, but no one remembered the cameras had done so. With your permission, Attorney General, let me try to explain."

"Be my guest, Mr. Morris. I'm well aware that you were the veterinarian on the Three R's Committee during the PRT experiments. The floor is yours."

"Gentlemen, each of us at this table knows we're dealing with extraordinary, almost unimaginable events here. We've figured out, at least to an extent, how the aura of the lab rat Larry and the presence emanating from the sentient entity within R-Five came to be. We also understand, again just to an extent, the whispering ability of Aubrey Adams. But the capabilities of Rohan Karteray—I'll call him that because I prefer to use his real name—are on an entirely different level.

"In fact," Morris continued, "he caused Miss Byers, me, and everyone else involved in Professor Tompkins's experiment to forget all about it. Karteray did that because he didn't want any human other than himself to try PRT until its side effects could be eliminated. He also made the techs who were monitoring the security cameras completely forget that the cameras showed he was giving himself shots."

Doctor Schwartz, whose hand-wavers, led by Moxus, had created the aura, and Robert Tompkins, whose PRT had morphed into the presence, decided to say nothing unless they were directly asked. Although the immunity they'd been granted covered anything they might say, they still worried that the enormity of what had happened would result in felony charges. They thought it best to remain silent because thousands of people had died and eventually someone would be made to pay.

"To put it plainly," Morris said, "Rohan Karteray injected himself with so much PRT that the entity into which it morphed enables him to travel not just into the fifth dimension, but also into the sixth and maybe beyond. I'm not sure where he's hiding now, but I suspect it's in another dimension."

"That can't be possible," CDC Director Friedman said, his jaw dropping.

"Why not?" Morris responded. "A month ago, none of us believed the aura, the presence, telepathy or even a self-adjusting insulin like PRT were possible either. Anyone here doubt that now?"

They all looked at him for a long while, dumbfounded.

Totally unable to refute Morris, Friedman asked, "Speaking of the aura and the presence, do we know where the lab rats Larry and Five are?"

Becky answered, "Last time I looked, day before yesterday, they were both in their cage barely breathing. I don't think either one of them will last much longer."

Hearing that, to no one's dismay, the attorney general seemed relieved, but glancing around the room, he realized that yet another person who had been subpoenaed wasn't there. His next question was, "Where's Aubrey Adams?"

*

And where was Aubrey? She was with Five and Larry now, on the Penobscot Indian reservation in Maine. She'd brought their hideously wounded six-inch bodies with her. Moxus, despite his frailty, was able to rise from his nursing home bed and drag himself to her side.

Her anger having subsided, she could not let Larry or Five suffer. She was gently whispering to them. Moxus assisted, using whatever was left of his long-ago-dissipated energy-healing powers.

Larry's fur began to grow thick and lustrous. Five's teeth sharpened, and an amused smile began taking form on his usually dull and blank face.

Their mouths began to move as if they were talking. Aubrey could have sworn they were.

She'd taken to heart the declaration of the biblical prophet, Isaiah: ". . I have had enough of the offerings of . . well-fed beasts; I do not delight in the blood of bulls, or of lambs, or of goats." *Or of Larry and R-Five,* she thought to herself.

And slowly, *they were healing.*

Chapter 38

Simona Gupta walked to the podium in the largest lecture hall at Harvard University, which the California-based think tank Milken Institute had ranked as the world's number one biotech research university. She had brought with her the security camera DVDs that Becky Beyers had played for Tom Garret, Bob Morris, and the others at the meeting convened by Mayor Perkins. Included was the DVD that showed Larry escaping from his cage, walking like a person, and making humanlike facial expressions, and the one that showed Rohan Karteray injecting himself with massive doses of PRT.

The topic Gupta had been asked to lecture on was diabetes research on nonhuman primates, but by now it was widely known that she'd tested PRT on her son, and rumors of his claimed abilities had spread across the world like wildfire.

Physicists, astronomers, and all the superstars of the biotech world were in attendance, including eighty-seven-year-old James Watson, codiscoverer with Francis Crick of the double helix structure of DNA, and Craig Venter, who founded the Human Genome Project and was the first to create a synthetic living organism. Also in attendance, of course, were Professor Robert Tompkins, creator of the world's first self-adjusting insulin, and Doctor Gary Schwartz, the first to use energy medicine to heal hemorrhaging blood vessels in lab animals.

Gupta's audience, for the most part, was skeptical, arrogant, and unwilling to accept outlandish theories about Rohan's supposedly incredible skills. Some of the older, more experienced researches would hear her out, but many thought the rumors they'd heard were sheer bunk.

Gupta began by saying, "Although my topic is diabetes research on apes, I want to describe some related developments that are, for lack of a better word, *fantastica*—" Before she could finish even that first sentence, hecklers interrupted.

A physicist from MIT shouted, "Professor Gupta, I hear your son's hanging out in the fifth and sixth dimensions these days."

Another, from Stanford, sneering, said, "Give us his address so we can send postcards."

And another from Kyoto University, Japan, yelled, "I saw that episode on *The Jetsons* when I was ten."

Their childish comments disturbed Gupta, but she was not surprised. She tried again. "Let me at least tell you—no, show you—the evidence."

But a woman from Technische Universität, Munich, whom Gupta knew said, "Simona, you and I have met many times. I've taken an interest in your work as you have in mine. Your development of a sign language to communicate with lab primates and testing diabetes cures on them has fascinated me. I've followed your experiments closely. But travel along wormholes? into other dimensions? Are you serious? Physics, madam, is not your field; it's mine. And I say that your claims, given existing technology, are not science based but are nonsense."

Another physicist, from Technion, Israel Institute of Technology, stood up. "Well, Professor Gupta, you and I have never met, but I know your work. I must say, although I don't mean to intentionally insult you, your claims seem absurd. As I understand it, your proof is some films of intelligent-looking lab rats that were injected with PRT, and a few conversations with your son after he injected himself with massive doses of it. This PRT obviously had some sort of effect, but interdimensional and wormhole travel? Please!"

From the University of California–Santa Barbara, a young astronomer who'd published several articles on the limits of intergalactic space travel shouted, "Professor, I'm going to tell you what I and just about everyone here thinks of your claims: they're insane!"

Just then Gupta signaled a technician to dim the lights and start the DVDs. The audience was intrigued. Their eyes focused. They saw Larry with his thick and lustrous, chestnut colored fur, penetrating large eyes, and a humanlike expression on his face. Some of them gasped; perspiration wetted most of their brows. All became silent. They watched!

The technician pressed pause precisely at the point where Larry, after escaping his cage and walking haughtily erect on his two hind legs, hopped atop a cabinet to study a map on the wall. They saw, beyond a doubt, that he could read the legend and every word. Next, he began altering the very physiology of his two front paws until they transformed, before their eyes, into perfectly shaped hands.

No one heckled Gupta anymore. She said, "Colleagues and friends, as scientists, we have been forced by new discoveries to change our concept of that which is possible many times. Michael Faraday's electromagnetism, Albert Einstein's relativity, Max Planck's quantum mechanics, and the theory of strings. You know the list."

At that moment, Rohan Karteray materialized, as if from thin air, alongside Simona on the dais. He had injected himself with so much of Tompkins's new insulin that even she didn't know the true extent of what he was capable of.

She signaled the technician, and again the DVD whirled. It showed Larry standing at the door to the cage of the female he desired, his perfectly shaped hands unhooking the latch, and with humanlike expressions constantly on his face. It also showed R-Five, while still in cage 28, suddenly disappearing from view as if he had vanished somehow into another dimension.

Simona caught Rohan's eyes and looked toward him lovingly. Suddenly, as if from a different layer of the universe, another Rohan materialized in the center of the auditorium. Everyone could plainly see there were two Rohans now, who were one and the same, standing in two different places at the same time.

"And for your consideration, ladies and gentlemen ..."

They stared agape at the Rohan standing next to Simona on the stage and at the same Rohan standing amid them in the center of the room.

Gupta surveyed her audience.

"... I submit this to you."

Epilogue

On the Brink of the Incredible

None of the extraordinary forces in play described in *The Leviticus Rats Experiment* or their effects are beyond the possible. Superintelligence, telepathy, other dimensions, travel through wormholes, extraterrestrial life, altering our physiology, and living in good health for hundreds of years are no longer just the imaginings of science fiction. We are on the brink of the incredible.

Superhuman Intelligence

There is such a thing as superhuman intelligence, and persons who possess it (such as Larry, although he is only a rat) have more powerful memories, better calculation skills, greater reasoning ability, and superior learning capacity, way beyond even genius level. They are able to come up with unique and innovative ideas and frequently have extraordinary talents be they human calculators, able to solve math problems as fast as computers; language prodigies, able to master multiple foreign tongues in incredibly short periods of time; or music virtuosos, able to instantly recall from a note or two hundreds of musical pieces and often perform them will dazzling skill.

Scientists have studied such people and have found that their brains are usually wired differently than most others'. Many have larger, denser gray matter and brain neurons that fire more rapidly, and sometimes their left and right cerebral hemispheres are directly connected to each other. At the very least, they're able to tap into the right hemisphere much more deeply than the rest of us can.

The left hemisphere is the logical, calculating, and planning side; the right, the artistic, emotional, and creative side. The left hemisphere is dominant, but emotions and thoughts from the right hemisphere, our subconscious side, often intrude. Those feelings frequently nag at us and disturb us. They make us wonder whether the choices we have made related to our career and our lifestyle were correct because such choices, although rational to the left hemisphere, may not fit for the true person that the right hemisphere tells us we are.

Persons with abnormal brain structure, such as those who've suffered serious brain injuries or whose left and right hemispheres are not separate but connected, are sometimes *idiot savants*, that is, idiots in most areas of human endeavor, but savants—geniuses—in one or more. Many have severe mental disorders but such disorders sometimes reveal the brain's most amazing abilities.

Doctor Allan Snyder of the Centre for the Mind at the University of Sydney in Australia has asked: "Does the normal human brain have latent savant-like abilities? Do our higher cognitive functions somehow block those abilities? And can we have savant-like abilities without the accompanying autism and other developmental disorders?" He has suggested that temporarily impairing the left hemisphere's frontotemporal lobes using low-impact magnetic pulses could result in savant-like mental powers. Such impairment would allow thoughts from the right hemisphere's frontotemporal lobes to emerge.

Research like Dr. Snyder's may one day enable us to boost our intellect to previously unheard-of levels. But already, there have been scores of known savants in the world whose superhuman mental powers are so astonishing that they're almost beyond belief.

Some of the most remarkable are women, but you will notice immediately from the following list that savant syndrome occurs much more often in males than in females. The reason for this may be that damage to the brain's left hemisphere can be produced by circulating testosterone, which in male fetuses reaches very high levels and is occasionally neurotoxic. Moreover, in the developing human fetus, the left hemisphere always completes its development later than the right and prebirth, therefore, is exposed for a longer period of time to testosterone induced damage. Researchers believe that this prolonged exposure of the left hemisphere to testosterone partly accounts for the highly disproportionate male-to-female ratio seen in disorders such as stuttering, dyslexia, hyperactivity, and autism. In fact, savant syndrome occurs in as high as 10 percent of individuals with autism, and males, given the developmental damage their left hemispheres sometimes suffer, are autistic far more frequently than females.

Nevertheless, the very word *savant*, meaning someone of extraordinary learning, is the family name of a woman who, although not possessed of superhuman mental abilities like idiot savants, was considered one of the world's most intelligent persons in her day.

Marilyn vos Savant (b. 1946) is an American columnist, author, lecturer, and playwright who rose to fame because of her listing from 1986 through 1989 in the *Guinness Book of World Records* as being the person with the world's highest IQ. On the Stanford-Binet test, second revision, she scored 228.

She was born Marilyn Mach in St. Louis, Missouri. Her parents were Joseph Mach and Marina vos Savant, and she is a descendant of physicist Ernst Mach, who calculated the ratio of the speed of a projectile to the speed of sound, v_p/v_s, which is now called the Mach number.

Since 1986 she has written "Ask Marilyn," a *Parade* magazine Sunday column, where she solves logical, mathematical, and vocabulary puzzles posed by readers and answers questions on a dizzying multitude of subjects.

She is a member of all the IQ societies, including the Mega Society, which requires intelligence levels that are reachable by only one out of every one million people.

In 1987 she married Robert Jarvik, developer of the Jarvik-7 artificial heart, and soon became chief financial officer of his company. She has served on the board of directors of the National Council on Economic Education, on the advisory boards of the National Association for Gifted Children and the National Women's History Museum, and as a fellow of the Committee for Skeptical Inquiry.

As impressive as the intellectual accomplishments of Marilyn vos Savant are, however, it is the capabilities of the idiot savants that astound us.

Laurence Kim Peek (1951–2009), on whose life the Dustin Hoffman character in the movie *Rain Man* is based, was born with profound brain damage. He was so disabled that he had difficulty walking; could not button his shirt, tie his shoes, or comb his hair; and scored well below average on IQ tests.

But what Kim could do was astonishing. "Kimputer," as he was called, read thousands of books and could read two pages at once. His left eye read the left page, and his right eye read the other. It took him three seconds to read the two pages, and he remembered everything printed on them. Kim memorized facts and trivia from multiple subject areas including history, geography, the arts, sports, and science. If you told him a date, he could instantly tell you what day of the week it fell on and what happened that day in minute detail. He could also recall every note, no matter how subtle, in every piece of music he had ever heard.

Leslie Lemke (b. 1952) was born with severe birth defects that required doctors to remove his eyes. His mother couldn't provide the care he needed, and a nurse named May Lemke adopted him when he was six months old.

As a child, Leslie had to be force-fed to teach him how to swallow. He could not stand until he was twelve. At fifteen, he finally learned how to walk when May Lemke strapped his body to hers to teach him, step by step.

At sixteen, he bloomed. May woke up one night and found Leslie playing Tchaikovsky's Piano Concerto No. 1. Leslie, who had no classical music training, was playing the piece flawlessly after having heard it just once on TV.

From then on, Leslie began playing all styles of music from ragtime to classical. Like the Tchaikovsky piece, he only has to hear the music one time to play it perfectly. He has become world famous and performs concerts to this day many times per year before amazed audiences.

Alonzo Clemons (b. circa 1958) was always good with his hands. At the age of two, he was drawn to Play-Doh, sculpting and molding it for hours at a time. When he was three, Clemons fell and sustained a serious head injury that changed him forever. For years, he was unable to speak, tie his shoes, or dress himself. Doctors determined he had an IQ of 40. The only time Clemons seemed to come alive was when he held a piece of clay.

Now, Clemons can look at any animal for just a few moments and then, without sculpting tools and using just his hands, create an astonishingly detailed 3D replica out of clay or wax. And while he sculpts, he never looks at the animal, relying only on his memory for reference. The images retained by his mind, with his very precise sense of touch on the clay, are so accurate that he can even sculpt in the dark. For years his work was based on photographs, which lent a static, vacant style to his pieces. But when he began visiting zoos and horse stables, observing animals in motion, his sculptures became masterpieces.

At about the same time, Clemons showed signs of improvement in everyday abilities. He began talking, albeit only in short phrases, but his progression over the years has enabled him to hold down a part-time job and learn to take care of himself. Eventually he took up another hobby, power lifting, a sport he participates in at the Special Olympics.

Elin Boudreaux (b. 1957), like Leslie Lemke, is a blind autistic savant, but with exceptional musical abilities. She can play a piece of music perfectly after hearing it once, and she has such a huge repertoire of songs in her head that when a newspaper reporter once tried to stump her by requesting that she play some obscure melodies, he failed miserably. She knew them all.

Ellen has two other savant skills that are unusual. First, despite her blindness, she is able to walk around without ever bumping into things. As she walks, she makes chirping sounds that seem to act like sonar, similar to the way bats use sonar, a.k.a. echolocation, to locate insects and feed upon them in the dark.

Second, Ellen has a meticulously precise digital clock ticking in her mind. When Ellen was eight years of age, to help overcome her fear of using a telephone, her mom coaxed her to listen to the automatic telephone recording of Jane Barbe, the "time lady." Every day until Barbe's death in 2003, millions of people heard her prerecorded voice, which telephone companies around the world used to tell callers the time, tell the temperature, give a weather report, read the horoscopes, and deliver messages like "The number you have dialed is unavailable."

From then on, miraculously, Ellen Boudreaux knew the exact hour and minute at any time of day without having ever seen a clock because she was blind.

Gottfried Mind (b. 1768) was one of the earliest savants in history. In 1776, his parents enrolled the eight-year-old Gottfried in an art academy, where his teachers noted that he was "very weak, incapable of hard work, but full of talent for drawing, a strange creature full of artist caprices along with a certain roguishness."

One day, Gottfried's mentor, a painter named Sigmund Hendenberger, was drawing a cat when Gottfried exclaimed, "That is no cat!" The teacher asked whether he could do better and sent him to a corner to draw. The cat the eight-year-old drew was so lifelike that Gottfried became known as "the cats' Raphael."

In the course of his narrow life spent indoors, he had worked himself into an almost paternal relation with domestic animals, particularly cats. While Gottfried was painting, a cat could often be seen sitting on his back or shoulder, and many times he kept the most awkward postures so he wouldn't disturb it. Frequently there'd be a second cat sitting by him, watching how the work went on. Frogs in a terrarium floated beside his easel with rabbits and birds nearby. With all these creatures, he kept up a most playful, loving, and intimate style of conversation so that his paintings captured not just their appearances but also their very personalities.

Sabine (b. 1904?) lived a perfectly normal, healthy, and happy life up until she entered school age at six. That year, she contracted typhoid fever, which caused convulsions, followed by an extended period of unconsciousness. The illness left her blind, mute, and with a childlike personality that she never outgrew. Over time, her sight returned, as did a low level of speech function, but she was incapable of taking care of herself.

Around age thirteen, Sabine became interested in coins and buttons. For some reason she preferred separating these items into groups of sixteen.

Sabine's disabilities were so severe that doctors tried to use this odd interest in the number 16 to teach her more advanced arithmetic so she could do things like keep track of the passage of time, learn the value of money, and make simple measurements. They soon realized, however, that she could perform astonishingly more complex calculations with ease. She could, for example, square any number from 11 to 99 in 10 seconds or less. When asked to calculate 23 × 23, she would almost immediately answer 529. But what surprised researchers most was her ability to solve problems in a unique way by somehow integrating her beloved number 16. So, when she answered 529, she would also point out that 529 was the same as 33 × 16 + 1. For 14 × 14, she could quickly answer 196, and then promptly follow it up with, "Or twelve times sixteen plus four."

Daniel Tammet (b. 1979) is a highly functioning autistic savant with exceptional mathematical and language abilities. He first became famous when he recited from memory *pi* to 22,514 decimal places to raise funds for the National Society for Epilepsy.

He has a rare form of synesthesia and sees numbers up to ten thousand as each having its own unique shape, color, texture, and feel. He can "see" the result of a math calculation, and he can "sense" whether a number is prime. Daniel has drawn what *pi* looks like to him: a rolling landscape full of different shapes and colors.

Daniel speaks eleven languages, one of which is Icelandic. In 2007, a Channel 5 documentary challenged him to learn the language in a week. Seven days later, Daniel was successfully interviewed in Icelandic on Icelandic TV.

When he was four years old, Daniel had bouts of epilepsy that, along with his autism, seemed to have brought about his savant abilities. Though he appears normal, Daniel contends that he actually had to will himself to learn how to talk to people and behave around them.

There is an important difference between Daniel Tammet and all the world's other prodigious savants: Daniel can tell you how he does what he does, and that makes him invaluable to scientists trying to understand savant syndrome.

Marilu Henner (b. 1952), costar of the long-running TV show *Taxi*, is not a savant, but no list of persons with superior mental ability would be complete without mentioning her. In 2012 she explained to CBS's *60 Minutes* how her highly superior autobiographical memory, or H-SAM, allows her to hold onto even the most minor of moments.

"Every single thing that you have ever done is on your hard drive," she explained. And it all can be retrieved.

Henner's skill came naturally, but she claimed, "By revisiting experiences and events in your life, you can train your brain"—and drastically improve your memory.

Henner suggested to start by identifying what she calls a "dominant track."

"Your track is something you remember exceptionally well. It's probably something you love to talk about; people have a travel track, a sports track, and a relationship track."

Once a track has been identified, simple things like music, photographs, smells, and tastes can be used to trigger memories of past events.

"Every once in a while, take a mental snapshot. *Where am I?* Pay attention, close your eyes, and listen to what's going on around you. At night, when you're brushing your teeth, sort of mentally go through your day," Henner says.

She's also suggested adding "juice" to your day, that is, get excited about it, because memory is tied to adrenaline.

"You can, like, do the laundry, do the kitty litter, go to the dentist. Or you could *do the laundry*! Take pride in it," she said.

Orlando Serrell (b. 1969) wasn't born autistic, and his savant skills only came about after a brain injury. At age ten, he was playing baseball when the ball struck him hard on the left side of his head. He fell to the ground but seemed uninjured and eventually got up to continue playing.

Afterward, for a while, Orlando had headaches. When they went away, he realized he had new abilities: he could perform complex calendar calculations and remember what the weather was like every day from the date of the accident forward.

Toss out any date since his accident—say, February 28, 1990—and almost immediately Serrell will tell you what day of the week that date fell on (this one was a Wednesday). He can even tell you what the weather was like that day in Virginia where he lives.

He hasn't memorized calendars or any kind of complicated algorithms in order to perform these feats; he says he can just see the answers in front of him. Apart from his unusual abilities, Serrell will be the first to admit he's a pretty average guy.

What makes Orlando Serrell so unique is that he may hold the key that unlocks the genius in us all. He did not possess any special skills until he was struck in the head. And his extraordinary gifts seem to be the only side effect. Could this mean once a key hemisphere in the brain is stimulated, we can all attain the level of genius he possesses and beyond? Only time and research will tell.

Stephen Wiltshire (b. 1974 in London) was mute, diagnosed as autistic, and sent to a school for special needs children. He did not utter a complete sentence until age five. Throughout his early childhood, he communicated almost only through his drawings. He had no training, but at age ten Wiltshire drew what he called *London Alphabet*, a group of drawings of structures from Albert Hall to London Zoo with the House of Parliament and the Imperial War Museum thrown in. He drew all the structures in minute detail. This body and his other works were so remarkable that in 1987 Wiltshire was part of a BBC program, *The Foolish Wise Ones*, during which, on camera, he drew an incredibly accurate sketch of St. Pancras Station, which he had visited for the first time only several hours before. As the cameras recorded, he quickly reproduced the elaborate and complicated building exactly as he had seen it, with the clock hands set at twenty minutes past eleven o'clock, the precise time he had viewed them.

Wiltshire's talent is that he can look at a subject for a few moments and then draw an incredibly detailed picture of it. He frequently draws entire cities from memory based on brief helicopter rides. He's been called "the Human Camera."

In May 2005 Stephen produced an immense panoramic memory drawing of Tokyo on a thirty-three-foot-long canvas within seven days following a short helicopter ride. Since then he has drawn Rome, Hong Kong, Frankfurt, Madrid, Dubai, Jerusalem, and London on giant canvases. When Wiltshire took the helicopter ride over Rome, he drew the city in such great detail that he included the exact number of columns in the Pantheon.

In October 2009 Stephen completed the last work in the series of panoramas, an eighteen-foot memory drawing of his "spiritual home," New York City. Following a twenty-minute helicopter ride, he sketched the view of New Jersey, Manhattan, the Financial District, Ellis Island, the Statue of Liberty, and Brooklyn over a period of five days at the Pratt Institute College of Art and Design in Manhattan.

In 2010, he made a series of drawings of Sydney, Australia, and of Hamilton, Bermuda, and the sale of those drawings broke auction records. In June of the same year, Christie's auctioned off his oil painting *Times Square at Night* for an unexpected huge sum.

A 2011 project in New York City involved Wiltshire's creation of a two-hundred-fifty-foot long panoramic memory drawing of New York, which is now displayed on a giant billboard at JFK Airport. It is a part of a global advertising campaign for the Swiss bank UBS, whose theme is "We Will Not Rest."

And the list above is only a partial inventory of his drawings. To list everything Stephen Wiltshire has done would take two more pages.

Tony Cicoria (b. 1952), an orthopedic surgeon, was hanging up the receiver of a pay phone in 1994 when lightning from a gathering storm cloud struck the booth, shooting through the phone and into his head. Luckily, a woman who'd been waiting to use the phone was a nurse and she performed CPR, saving his life. After a few weeks, Cicoria recovered, and everything seemed to return to normal.

Shortly afterward, he had a mysterious, insatiable need to listen to classical piano music, but he soon found that just listening to the music wasn't cutting it. So, despite never before having shown any desire to play an instrument, he bought sheet music and began teaching himself the piano. Learning was slow going though, because instead of playing the Chopin composition in front of him, he kept wanting to play the melodies that were echoing inside his head. When he realized these songs were of his own creation, he began furiously writing them down until he had dozens composed. In 2008, Cicoria released a CD of his music called *Notes from an Accidental Pianist and Composer*. His best-known song from the album is fittingly titled "The Lightning Sonata."

Tommy McHugh (1949–2012), a British artist and poet, was in the bathroom getting ready for work as a carpenter when he suddenly felt a sharp pain in his head. Blood began running out his nose, eyes, and ears, and he collapsed to the floor. It took five hours for surgeons to stop the bleeding from two aneurysms, but miraculously, he survived. When he returned home, McHugh, with no previous interest whatsoever in the arts, was overtaken by a powerful urge to create.

It began with scribbled poetry that filled notebooks, then drawings flowed out of him without any conscious thought. But he truly found his outlet when he started painting.

McHugh's artwork is made up primarily of faces that he describes as his personality crying for help to save him from his obsession. McHugh has said the images in his mind change so rapidly that by the time he's started painting, the one image has been replaced by another, which he feels compelled to paint as well. Because of the constantly evolving pictures in his head, his home is covered in paintings—on canvases, on the walls, even on the ceiling and floor. When he runs out of space to paint, he simply covers previous works. He estimates there are some areas of his house with a layer of paint three inches thick, hiding dozens of pieces underneath.

His compulsion keeps him painting an average of eighteen hours a day, seven days a week. He recently opened a gallery with artwork for sale to help support himself and his uncontrollable obsession.

Other Dimensions

String theory, difficult for even physicists to understand, predicts that as many as eleven dimensions exist. In fact, most of string theory's equations don't work unless there are at least that many, because there's just not enough room in the four dimensions we're familiar with—height, width, length, and time—for them to work. It is a conceptual framework in which the infinitesimally small particles of matter and energy such as quarks, gluons, photons, and Higgs bosons are replaced by one-dimensional objects called strings. The theory says that all the different particles scientists have discovered arise from different vibrations of these strings. If, for example, a string vibrates at a particular speed and in a particular direction, it might become a quark. If it vibrates at a different speed and in another direction, its quantum state changes and it might become a Higgs boson or a gluon. Also, in addition to the kinds of particles postulated by the standard model of particle physics, string theory incorporates gravity via a new theoretical particle called a graviton. Therefore, the theory is a candidate for a theory of everything, a self-contained model that describes all fundamental forces, forms of energy, and forms of matter.

In the early twentieth century, the long-believed smallest building block of everything, the atom, was proven to consist of even smaller components called protons, neutrons, and electrons, which are the largest subatomic particles. In the 1970s, it was discovered that protons and neutrons are themselves made up of even smaller particles such as the above-mentioned quarks, gluons, and Higgs bosons. Quantum theory is the set of rules that describes the interactions of these particles.

In the 1980s, string theory emerged. It showed how all subatomic particles and all forms of energy and matter could be constructed by hypothetical one-dimensional "strings," infinitesimally small building blocks that have only the dimension of length, but not of height or width.

Moreover, string theory suggests that the universe is made up of multiple dimensions. Height, width, and length constitute three-dimensional space, and time gives us a total of four observable dimensions, but string theory supports the possibility of ten dimensions, the remaining six of which we cannot detect directly. This was later increased to eleven dimensions based on various interpretations of the ten-dimensional theory, which eventually led to five partial theories that all seem correct.

The "strings" vibrate in multiple dimensions, and depending on the speed and direction of their vibrations, which determines the type of subatomic particles they become, they may be seen in three-dimensional space as matter (i.e., atoms, which are composed of protons, neutrons, and electrons), or light, which is a form of energy (photons), or gravity (gravitons)—and all gravity and every form of matter and energy is the result of these vibrations.

But scientists were not comfortable with the many different theories, which all appeared mathematically correct yet described the same thing. After the first version of string theory equations was formulated, another version of equations was discovered, then another, and then another. Eventually, as mentioned, there were five major ones. The main difference between each was principally the number of dimensions in which the strings developed, and their characteristics. Some strings were open loops, some were closed loops, some were double loops, and so forth.

In 1994, Edward Witten of the Institute for Advanced Study in Princeton, New Jersey, and other researchers suggested that the five different versions of string theory might be describing the same thing seen from different perspectives. They proposed a unifying theory called "M-theory", the *M* standing for membrane. M-theory brought all the string theories together by asserting that strings are really one-dimensional slices of two-dimensional membranes vibrating in eleven-dimensional space. (I told you it is hard to understand, even for physicists.)

As demonstrated in *The Leviticus Experiment*, visualizing a world consisting of just four dimensions—height, width, length, plus *time*—which gave rise to the concept of space-time, is difficult, and conceptualizing one with an additional fifth dimension is almost impossible, let alone conceptualizing one with eleven (or figuring out what a one-dimensional slice of a two-dimensional membrane looks like). If string theory and M-theory are correct, however, that's the shape of the world we live in. We simply can't perceive it.

The physicists who devised string theory and M-theory, which are still untested experimentally, can't really perceive that many dimensions either, that is, picture them in their minds, although their mathematics tells them these dimensions must exist. Remember, however, that only a few centuries ago most people believed the earth was flat because they couldn't see its curvature beyond the horizon. Like them, we are unable to see beyond our "horizon," so for now we'll have to accept *on faith* that the many dimensions that string theory predicts but that no one can actually see or feel are really out there.

I'm not getting religious on you. We had to accept on faith the prediction of Albert Einstein's general theory of relativity that time slows down as one approaches the speed of light. That prediction, however, has been repeatedly confirmed as accurate. When atomic clocks, which are able to measure the passage of time in units as small as a 10^{18} of a second, have been placed on spacecraft traveling at speeds of forty thousand miles per hour and then compared to atomic clocks on Earth, the clocks didn't match. The clocks returning from space showed that less time had passed on the spacecraft than on Earth.

Traveling at the Speed of Light and Faster

Physicists have developed a way in which a spacecraft might be able to travel faster than the speed of light without breaking any of the laws of Einstein's general theory of relativity. The basic idea would be to surround a spacecraft within a man-made bubble of energy that would contract the space in front of the craft and expand the space behind. To visualize this, imagine yourself in a room and walking across a carpet to reach a table. Instead of walking across the carpet, you could lasso the table and drag it toward you, causing the carpet between you and the table to bunch up. You'd have moved very little in the room, and instead the space in front of you would have shrunk. This expansion/contraction drive would change the very geometry of space. The spaceship would not move within the man-made energy bubble but instead would be carried along as the bubble region itself moved forward because of the actions of the drive.

By this method, the spaceship would never be traveling faster than light inside the bubble, but would be moving far faster relative to observers outside it.

This type of travel has been dubbed "Alcubierre warp drive" in honor of physicist Miguel Alcubierre of the University of Mexico, who was the first to write about it. He theorized that by using his method, such a craft could achieve a relative speed of up to ten times the speed of light.

Alcubierre warp drive, however, is very speculative, and the bubble it proposes would need to be a configurable energy field with density lower than a vacuum's, that is, with negative mass. Such a thing is possible, but that is a discussion beyond the scope of *The Leviticus Experiment* and beyond the ability of this author to explain or understand.

Another way of arriving at a destination faster than light would be to travel through wormholes, as Larry did in this story. Again, however, wormhole travel would not involve attaining speeds faster than light but would, rather, be travel through shortcuts in space-time.

Telepathy

Is telepathy, which is the direct transfer of thought from one person to another, possible? Can we communicate through thought alone like Larry, R-Five, and the Luna Gigantica 12 queen in this story? Maybe. But to date, all persons who've claimed to be telepaths have failed to demonstrate it in strictly controlled laboratory experiments. They've been repeatedly exposed as charlatans.

On the other hand, all of us emanate auras, causing the question to arise as to whether these auras can somehow be amplified and used as a channel of thought communication. That such auras, which are actually biochemically generated energy fields, really exist is beyond doubt. We know, as discussed in *The Leviticus Experiment*, that the auras emanated by energy healers can interact with and affect the auras of their patients. In addition, experiments designed by the real Doctor Gary Schwartz, chairman of the Laboratory for Advances in Consciousness and Health at the University of Arizona, have shown that the aura interaction among close family members, especially between mothers and their children, is particularly powerful.

Why this is so is not fully known, but researchers believe the genetic similarity of their biochemically generated energy fields is a big part of it.

At the most basic level, all forms of matter and of energy, including the auras emanated by living things, are composed of the miniscule particles that make up atoms. In certain pairs, these particles, even when separated by great distances, can instantly "know" what the other is doing. Subatomic particles have a quality known as spin, and according to quantum theory, the moment you change the spin of one particle, its sister particle, no matter how distant, will immediately begin spinning at the same speed too. This phenomenon, first predicted and called "spooky" by Einstein, was demonstrated at the University of Geneva in 1997 when physicists sent photons seven miles in opposite directions and found that interfering with one provoked an instantaneous response in the other.

The weird way entangled particles stay connected even when separated by large distances was reconfirmed by physicists at the University of Vienna in 2013. The results from their experiment demonstrated again that a pair of "entangled particles," once their spin is measured, can somehow instantly communicate with each other so that their states always match.

Maybe, since the subatomic particles of which children are made up are virtually the same as the subatomic particles of their mothers, children and their mothers always stay "entangled" and can therefore always be aware of the other's state.

This ability of particles to know what the other is doing, without seeing, hearing, smelling, touching, or feeling each other, is in essence a form of telepathic communication on a subatomic level. Moreover, since the communication is instantaneous, it somehow happens even faster than the speed of light.

But on a practical level, scientists have moved beyond even that. They've been able to insert a chip into the brains of patients who are totally paralyzed and connect it to a computer, so that through thought alone the patients can surf the web, read and write emails, play video games, control their wheelchairs, operate appliances, and manipulate mechanical arms.

And there is no reason why all of us can't do the same thing via implanted computer chips. That's more than telepathy; it's telekinesis, which is the ability to move objects by thought alone.

Immortality

No, we're not anywhere close to figuring out how to prevent ourselves from dying of old age, nor, unlike Larry, have we learned how to alter our physiology to significantly extend our life spans. The Hebrew Bible says that Methuselah died when he was 969, but to date the oldest documented person ever was Jeanne Calment of France (1875–1997), who died when she was 122.5. One day, however, in the not too distant future, we may discover a fountain of youth with an elixir that will give us immortality.

Antiaging Drugs

In the first case of a major pharmaceutical extending the life span of a mammal, scientists gave elderly mice rapamycin, a drug used to slow cell growth in cancer patients, and the rodents lived the mouse equivalent of thirteen extra years. Even longtime believers in longevity enhancement were stunned by the results, which were duplicated independently in multiple laboratories.

If rapamycin did the same for humans, then the average life span for a male in the United States would increase from 78 to 101, and for females from 83 to 106. However, it's unlikely rapamycin will be tested on human subjects until its severe side effects can be eliminated.

In part, rapamycin works by mimicking the effects of a calorie restriction (CR) diet, which has been shown to extend life span in some animals. Drugs that have been studied for possible longevity effects because of CR-mimic effect also include metformin and resveratrol. In some studies, calorie restriction has been shown to extend the life of even rhesus monkeys, and long-term human trials of CR-mimic drugs are now being done.

March 8, 2013
University of New South Wales

Drugs that combat aging may be available within five years. Landmark work finally demonstrates that a single antiaging enzyme in our bodies, *SIRT1*, can be targeted with the potential to prevent age-related diseases and extend life spans. *SIRT1* is switched on naturally by calorie restriction and exercise, but it can also be triggered by synthetic activators. The most common naturally occurring activator is resveratrol, which is found in small quantities in red wine, but man-made activators with much stronger activity are the focus of current research. Four thousand of these activators, many of which are a hundred times more potent than a glass of red wine, have already been developed.

Work published by researchers in the March 8, 2013, issue of *Science* shows that all the activation drugs tested work on *SIRT1* and other potential antiaging enzymes through a common mechanism. This means that a whole new class of antiaging drugs is now viable that could ultimately prevent cancer, Alzheimer's disease, type 2 diabetes, and a slew of other diseases.

"Ultimately, these drugs would treat one disease, but unlike drugs of today, they would prevent twenty others," says the lead author of the *Science* paper, Professor David Sinclair, a molecular geneticist and currently codirector of the Laboratories for the Biological Mechanisms of Aging at Harvard Medical School. "In effect, they would slow the aging process."

There have already been promising results in some trials with implications for cancer, cardiovascular disease, type 2 diabetes, Alzheimer's and Parkinson's disease, fatty liver disease, cataracts, osteoporosis, muscle wasting, sleep disorders, and inflammatory diseases such as psoriasis, arthritis, and colitis.

"In the history of pharmaceuticals, there has never been a drug that tweaks an enzyme to make it run faster. ... Our drugs can mimic the benefits of diet and exercise, but there is no impact on weight," says Professor Sinclair. In animal models, overweight mice given synthetic resveratrol were able to run twice as far as slim mice, and they lived 15 percent longer.

While any drug would be strictly prescribed for certain conditions, Sinclair suggests that one day they could be taken orally as a preventative. This would be in much the same way as statin drugs are commonly prescribed today to prevent, instead of simply treating, cardiovascular disease.

"Now we are looking at whether there are benefits for those who are already healthy. Things there are also looking promising," says Sinclair.

"We're finding that aging isn't the irreversible affliction that we thought it was. ... Some of us could live to one hundred and fifty, but we won't get there without more research."

Professor Sinclair formed a start-up company, SIRTRIS, to develop his antiaging technology, which was subsequently sold to the pharmaceutical giant GlaxoSmithKline. Professor Sinclair and many of his associates are now scientific advisors or otherwise employed at GSK.

June 2014
Katholieke University, at Leuven, Belgium

A study by Belgian doctoral researcher Wouter De Haes and colleagues provides new evidence that metformin, one of the world's most widely used antidiabetic drug, slows aging and increases life span.

In experiments reported in the journal *Proceedings of the National Academy of Sciences*, the researchers found that the mechanism behind metformin's age-slowing effects is that the drug causes an increase in the number of toxic oxygen molecules released in our cells and this, surprisingly, increases cell robustness and longevity.

Mitochondria—the energy factories in cells—use glucose digested down from the food we eat to generate tiny electric currents. Those currents provide our cells with energy. Highly reactive oxygen molecules, which can be toxic, are produced as a by-product of this process.

While these molecules are harmful because they can damage proteins and DNA and disrupt normal cell functioning, a small dose can actually do the cell good. "As long as the amount of harmful oxygen molecules released in the cell remains small, it has a positive long-term effect. Cells use the toxic reactive oxygen particles to their advantage before they can do any damage," explains Wouter De Haes. "Metformin causes a slight increase in the number of harmful oxygen molecules. We found that this makes cells stronger and extends their healthy life span."

It was long thought that harmful reactive oxygen molecules were the very cause of aging. The food and cosmetics industries are quick to emphasize the antiaging qualities of products containing antioxidants, such as skin creams, fruit and vegetable juices, red wine, and dark chocolate. But while antioxidants do in fact neutralize harmful reactive oxygen molecules in the cell, they actually negate metformin's antiaging effects because it relies entirely on these toxic molecules to work.

The researchers studied metformin's mechanism in the tiny roundworm *Caenorhabditis elegans*, an ideal species for studying aging because it has a life span of only three weeks. "As they age, the worms get smaller, wrinkle up, and become less mobile. But worms treated with metformin show very limited size loss and no wrinkling. They not only age slower, but also stay healthier longer," says Wouter De Haes. "While we should be careful not to overextrapolate our findings to humans, the study is promising as a foundation for future research."

So far, human tests have shown that metformin significantly suppresses some cancers and heart disease. Reformulated, it could be an effective drug for counteracting the debilitating effects of aging.

Nanotechnology

Nano is a prefix meaning one billionth, and a billionth of a meter is a nanometer. To give you an idea of just how small nanotechnology is, consider that the number of nanometers that could fit inside a marble equals the number of marbles it would take to fill the earth. To write such a number down would completely cover an 8.5" × 11" page. Scientists believe that in the future, nanotechnology will enable them to build infinitesimally small "nanorobots" that doctors will inject into us like vaccines and that'll patrol our organs, tissues, and blood vessels, giving rise to life extension by repairing diseased and aging cells.

The ideas and concepts behind nanoscience started with a talk entitled "There's Plenty of Room at the Bottom" by physicist Richard Feynman at the California Institute of Technology in 1959, long before the term *nanotechnology* was used. In his talk, Feynman described a process in which scientists would be able to manipulate and control individual atoms and molecules. More than a decade later, Professor Norio Taniguchi, in his explorations of ultraprecision machining, coined the term *nanotechnology*. It wasn't until 1981, with the development of the scanning tunneling microscope, which could "see" individual atoms, that modern nanotechnology began.

A mad dash by physicists and computer engineers to develop usable nanotechnology is currently under way because the absolute limit of how much digital information can be packed into a transistor is fast approaching. A transistor is a circuit that amplifies electrical signals and is the fundamental building block of all modern electronic devices. Transistors replaced the glass vacuum tubes many of us remember were in use when we were kids. Following its development in 1947, the transistor revolutionized electronics and paved the way for smaller and cheaper radios, calculators, and computers and a myriad of other devices.

Modern transistors are composed of silicon chips into which thousands of electrical circuits can be embedded. During the past several decades, scientists have been able to slice these silicon chips thinner and thinner and thereby pack more and more computer power into a smaller and smaller space. Your new cell phone has literally thousands of more gigabytes' capacity than the laptop you bought only five years ago. But a problem is on the horizon because we have sliced silicon chips just about as thin as they can get.

To overcome this problem, nanotechnologists are trying to build submolecule-size computers. With some success, using recently perfected scanning tunneling microscopes, they've been able to manipulate the atoms within molecules and even the subatomic particles of the atoms. Plans are on the drawing board to use certain kinds of atoms and their subatomic particles as components in nanometer-size computers. With such computers, nanotechnologists will build the above-described nanorobots, and the age of nanomedicine will be upon us.

Using nanorobots, the largest of which will be the size of a bacterium, doctors could treat everything from heart disease to cancer. Unlike with acute treatment, these robots would stay in a patient's body forever, rushing around in his or her veins, making corrections; repairing aging cells; healing wounds; damaged organs, and broken bones; and curing illnesses for which no cure is presently known, such as type 1 diabetes.

Body Part Replacement

Cloning and stem cell research could provide a way to generate cells, body parts, or even entire bodies that would be genetically identical to those of a prospective patient. Recently, the US Department of Defense initiated a program to research the possibility of growing human body parts on mice, but complex biological structures, such as mammalian joints and limbs, have not yet been replicated.

Dog and primate brain transplantation experiments were conducted in the mid-twentieth century but failed because of tissue rejection and the inability to restore nerve connections. As of 2006, however, the implantation of bioengineered bladders grown from patients' own cells has proven to be a viable treatment for bladder disease. Proponents of body part replacement and cloning contend that the required biotechnologies are likely to appear earlier than other life-extension technologies.

The use of human stem cells, particularly embryonic stem cells, has been extremely controversial. The objections of opponents of stem cell research are usually based on religious teachings, but proponents point out that cells are routinely formed and destroyed in a variety of contexts. Use of stem cells taken from umbilical cords or parts of the adult body has not provoked the same intense controversy.

Some cloning researchers predict that in the not too distant future we'll be able to produce whole bodies, lacking consciousness, the organs from which we'll use for transplantation into their genetically identical cloners whose own organs have become diseased or too old to properly function.

Modifying or Fooling Genes

Gene therapy, in which artificial or mutated genes are integrated with the natural genes in a living organism, has been proposed as a future strategy to prevent aging. Scientists at the Buck Institute for Research on Aging in Novato, California, combined mutations in roundworms, and the mutations set off a positive feedback loop in specific tissues, basically causing these worms to live to the human equivalent of four hundred to five hundred years.

A large number of other genetic modifications affecting biochemical processes have been reported to significantly extend life span in model organisms.

In *The Selfish Gene*, Richard Dawkins describes an approach to life extension first proposed by Peter Medawar that involves "fooling" genes into thinking the body is young. The basic idea is that our bodies are composed of genes that activate throughout our lifetimes, some when we are young, and others when we are older. It is thought that these genes are activated by environmental factors, and the changes caused by their activation as we grow older can be lethal. It is a statistical certainty that we possess more lethal genes that activate in later life than we do those that activate in early life. Therefore, to extend life, we should be able to prevent these genes from switching on, and we should be able to do this

191

by "identifying changes in the internal chemical environment of a body that take place during aging ... and by simulating the superficial chemical properties of a young body."

Do We Have Souls?

If the real Doctor Schwartz is correct, that our auras live on after our bodies perish, then those auras may be our souls, which religion tells us will join the souls of our loved ones in heaven when we die.

Life on Other Planets

Astronomers have come a long way since Gliese 581g, the first planet outside our solar system potentially able to support advanced life, was detected in 2010. In the constellation Libra, twenty light-years away, Gliese 581g was dubbed the Goldilocks Planet because it was thought to have an oxygen-rich atmosphere, to have water, and to have a temperature that was neither too cold nor too hot. Subsequent studies, however, failed to confirm these conditions.

The six-hundred-million-dollar Kepler space telescope came online in May 2009, but its observations ended in August 2013 when a mechanical failure made it impossible to aim the telescope accurately. By then Kepler had discovered more than half of all currently known exoplanets, and we know that most of the stars it photographed have planets orbiting them, with as many as one in five able to sustain life. That could add up to a staggering forty billion habitable worlds in our galaxy alone.

No longer able to fulfill its primary function, the Kepler space telescope's future is under review by NASA, and a proposal made at the 2014 Astrophysics Senior Review of Operating Missions that it continue hunting planets by employing a different technique is being considered.

Also, huge radio telescopes located in several continents have been wired together via computer, forming in effect one nearly Earth-sized radio dish listening for signals from intelligent civilizations. The data is collected by sophisticated software and then beamed via the internet to millions of laptops for analysis by amateur astronomers. Discouragingly, however, none of the data so far have revealed coherent patterns that might have been sent by intelligent life-forms. But Kepler is back online!

NASA finds "Earth's Bigger, Older Cousin"

Michael Pearson, CNN
Friday, July 24, 2015, updated 9:30 a.m. ET

NASA said Thursday that its Kepler spacecraft has spotted "Earth's bigger, older cousin": the first nearly Earth-size planet to be found in the habitable zone of a star similar to our own.

Though NASA can't say for sure whether the planet is rocky like ours or has water and air, it's the closest match yet found.

"Today, Earth is a little less lonely," Kepler researcher Jon Jenkins said.

The planet, Kepler-452b, is about fourteen hundred light-years from Earth in the constellation Cygnus. It's about 60 percent bigger than Earth, NASA says, and is located in its star's habitable zone—the region where life-sustaining liquid water is possible on the surface of a planet.

A visitor there would experience gravity about twice that of Earth's, and planetary scientists say the odds of it having a rocky surface are "better than even."

While it's a bit farther from its star than Earth is from the sun, its star is brighter, so the planet gets about the same amount of energy from its star as Earth does from the sun. And that sunlight would be very similar to Earth's, Jenkins said.

The planet "almost certainly has an atmosphere," Jenkins said, although scientists can't say what it's made of. But if the assumptions of planetary geologists are correct, he said, Kepler-452b's atmosphere would probably be thicker than Earth's, and it would have active volcanoes.

It takes 385 days for the planet to orbit its star, very similar to Earth's 365-day year, NASA said. And because it's spent so long orbiting in this zone—6 billion years—it's had plenty of time to brew life, Jenkins said.

"That's substantial opportunity for life to arise, should all the necessary ingredients and conditions for life exist on this planet," he said in a statement.

Before the discovery of this planet, one called Kepler-186f was considered the most Earthlike, according to NASA. That planet, no more than a tenth bigger than Earth, is about five hundred light-years away from us. But it gets only about a third of the energy from its star as Earth does from the sun, and noon there would look similar to the evening sky here, NASA says.

The six-hundred-million-dollar Kepler mission was launched in 2009 with a goal to survey a portion of the Milky Way for habitable planets. From a vantage point sixty-four million miles from Earth, it scans the light from distant stars, looking for almost imperceptible drops in a star's brightness, suggesting a planet has passed in front of it.

It has discovered more than a thousand planets. Twelve of those, including Kepler-425b, have been less than twice the size of Earth and in the habitable zones of the stars they orbit.

Missions are being readied to move scientists closer to the goal of finding yet more planets and cataloging their atmospheres and other characteristics.

In 2017, NASA plans to launch a planet-hunting satellite called TESS that will be able to provide scientists with more detail on the size, mass, and atmospheres of planets circling distant stars.

The next year, the James Webb Space Telescope will go up. That platform, NASA says, will provide astonishing insights into other worlds, including their color, seasonal differences, weather, and even the potential presence of vegetation.

A Cure for Diabetes

As to self-adjusting insulin, like Tompkins's PRT, despite all the recent advances in biomedicine and biotechnology, there is still no such thing. There are only several brands of insulin pumps, now widely available, that diabetics can attach by inserting a tube a quarter inch into their skin. These pumps can "self-adjust" and automatically change the amount of insulin delivered based on readings transmitted from a glucose sensor, which diabetics also attach to their skin. Together, these "insulin pump–glucose sensor" combinations are like artificial pancreases. When functioning properly, they release the right amount of insulin needed to metabolize whatever glucose a diabetic has digested down from the carbohydrates he's consumed.

They're far from perfect, but they're the closest we've come to curing type 1 diabetes short of surgical implant of insulin-producing cells from a healthy donor's pancreas. Type 2 diabetics, on the other hand, are often able to cure themselves by exercising, losing weight, and strictly controlling their diets.

In all the world's medical literature, however, there is not a single case of a type 1 diabetic doing that and naturally healing himself. To date, in fact, no type 1 has ever been fully cured. Although pancreas transplantation, if successful, can eliminate the need for insulin and return the individual to a more normal lifestyle, antirejection drug injections become necessary, instead of the no longer needed insulin shots.

Stem cell therapy holds immense promise. It has successfully produced glucose-responding beta cells that release insulin but has yet to cure any type 1 diabetic long term.

Diabetes is a worldwide epidemic that has sickened or killed tens of million people. It killed three times more each year on average than COVID.

Glossary

AALAS. American Association of Laboratory Animal Science.

AJCC. Acharya Jagadish Chandra College in Calcutta, India.

ALAT. Assistant laboratory animal technician.

ATOM. Advanced Trauma Operative Management, a medical school course in which live pigs are intentionally wounded, designed to provide training for medics sent to Iraq, Afghanistan, and elsewhere.

CDC. Centers for Disease Control and Prevention, a federal agency within the Department of Health and Human Services.

Difethialone. An anticoagulant used as a poison to kill rodents.

DVM. Doctor of veterinary medicine.

Feras 5. Nickname for *Rattus feras indomitus 5*, that is, wild untamed rat 5.

Gliese 581g. A planet orbiting a red dwarf star in the constellation Libra.

Gliese humanoid 581g. Giant, hairy, humanoid, apelike creatures inhabiting Gliese 581g.

Gliese rattus 581g. Ratlike creatures on Gliese 581g.

Indandione. An anticoagulant-type poison used to kill rodents.

LAT. Laboratory animal technician.

LATG. Laboratory animal technologist.

Luna Gigantica 12. Largest of the fictional twelve moons orbiting a giant planet in the Large Magellanic Cloud.

Luna rodenta gigantica 12. Big, rodent-like creatures on the fictional moon Luna Gigantica 12.

Mandius 481. a planet in the Andromeda Galaxy's Erhowe star system.

PETA. People for Ethical Treatment of Animals.

PRT. Self-adjusting insulin invented by Professor Robert Tompkins.

Rattus feras indomitus. Wild untamed rats.

Rattus feras indomitus 1, 2, 3, 4, and 5. Wild untamed rats nicknamed Feras 1, 2, 3, 4, and 5 in *The Leviticus Experiment.*

R-Five. Nickname for *Rattus norvegicus diabetica 5.*

Rattus indomitus Mandius 481 A, B, and C. Wild rats on the planet Mandius-481, nicknamed A, B, and C in *The Leviticus Experiment.*

Rattus norvegicus diabetica. Brown rats with diabetes.

Rattus norvegicus diabetica 1, 2, 3, 4, and 5. Brown rats with diabetes.

The Three R's. Guiding ethical principles for persons who work with lab animals used in biotechnological research: refine the experiments so they cause no pain; reduce the number of animals needed; and replace the animals with tissue samples or computer models whenever possible.

Type 1 diabetes. Autoimmune disease that attacks and kills insulin-producing cells in the pancreas.

Type 2 Diabetes. Disease caused when the pancreas can't produce enough insulin, often triggered by obesity and lack of exercise.

UVA. University of Arizona.

UVM. University of Vermont.

Vet Tech. Veterinary Technologist.

Printed in the United States
by Baker & Taylor Publisher Services.

Printed in the United States
by Baker & Taylor Publisher Services